Shimmering Bear

The Rohendra Complex, Book 3

Georgina Makalani

Also by Georgina Makalani

The Last Dragon Skin Chronicles
The Legend of Iski Flare
The Magics of Rei-Een
The Mark of Oldra
The Raven Crown

The Rohendra Complex:
The Dragonfly
Sparrow Song
Shimmering Bear
Rohendra Queen

One

O n the bridge of Colonel Calder's small ship, Isla Tarle looked out into the dark space surrounding them and then back to the display. "Dust," she murmured as she put her finger to the image that shone above the panel.

"Excuse me?" Calder asked, although he appeared to have lost the angry edge he usually carried. She studied him again, wondering just what this man was, what had caused him to become so, and what he might have been.

"Why did you choose that face?" she asked. "Why did you change?"

He shook his head as though not willing to answer her and turned his attention to the monitor.

"Dust," she repeated, her fingers moving through the image, willing it to show her what she needed. She was surprised when it did just that. "That is how they made it so dangerous." She was unsure how she knew that, but she did know more than she had known before. She was reminded of the Rohen sparkling in the dim light of the forest and taking her far away—and the feelings of certainty, understanding, and loss that had flooded through her.

"What are you talking about?" Calder asked, for the first time in too long reminding her of Kalli, the man he had been before.

"New name, new face, and yet I guess you are still the same man, no matter what Gray thinks."

He grunted something unintelligible. Isla took a deep breath and focused again on the monitor.

The three elongated asteroids slowly moved around each other in an odd dance across the black void of space. "Were they getting closer to a planet?" she asked.

He shook his head. "They haven't moved from this location. You need to explain the dust."

"They broke it up, whoever came to collect it, whoever worked out what they could do with it. They broke it into dust and took it to Rennet. That is why no one saw it, why no one realised what had been done."

"If the Rohen see as much as you claim they do, then they would have known something."

"Perhaps they couldn't get close enough," she mused. "Maybe they were avoiding something. Like they avoid you."

"That could be fear," he said, something smug in his smile.

"Of you or for you?" she asked.

His confidence shifted. He looked at her as though he wanted to ask more, but didn't.

"I don't know," she muttered. "I don't know where to go next or what I need to do."

"You found the containment, or at least the reason for it. Do you have to report in?"

"They know," she sighed, pulling her fingers from the image. It disappeared.

He opened his mouth and then closed it, sitting back in the pilot's seat.

"I don't know how I know that," she admitted. "Do you want to return to help Hendra?"

He looked at her and then back to the controls, his fingers on the panel. "She doesn't need me for this."

"Are you sure? Half the Complex appears to be rising up against her."

"Isn't that what you wanted?"

"No," she said.

"What do you want?" he asked, looking her in the eye for the first time in too long.

"To find Gray and make sure he is ok." *Ensure he survived,* she thought, remembering the crash of the building around her. If the stonework was filled with dust as she feared, the Rohen might not be able to reach him. Would he think to ask for their help?

"You know what she was, don't you?" he asked, but his focus was on the screen ahead of him.

"Alice? Not what I thought, if she is dead."

"If," Calder said, reaching out and gripping her arm too tightly. If she had been paying more attention, she would have been able to get out of the way. She tried not to pull from his hold. They had to work together—the Rohen had said he would help her. But she didn't want his hands on her, reminding her of someone he no longer was. Isla wasn't sure what she was working towards. She had done as she had been tasked, and she didn't want to admit she was feeling a little lost.

"If," he repeated, standing, and Isla felt more nervous. Then he was throwing himself into his seat, belting up. Isla did the same as he moved his fingers through the controls.

"Where are we going?"

"Rennet," he muttered.

"Is this to find what is left of the dust?" she asked. She might be unsure as to where to head next, but he was making her uncomfortable. "Or to get back to Hendra?"

"No, this is to check out a body."

"I would guess it is being very carefully checked over."

"Not closely enough. They think they have Alice. What if they don't?" he asked, turning to stare at her.

"You think Alice planted a body and ran. If that was the case, why would it have been dead for so long?"

"To put us off the scent. To make it look as though she is long gone."

"She might be," Isla said. "She might have been gone for so long that whoever or whatever took her place became... I don't know, it doesn't make sense."

"Yes, you do," he said, reaching out and poking her arm without turning from the controls.

"What?"

"The Rohen. It was you. It behaved like you—it knew what you knew."

"Because it called you Kalli?" Isla had to work to supress her smile as he nodded. It had unnerved him far more than she had realised. "It wasn't that good a likeness. Gray saw through it."

"Hendra is a busy woman. Distracted. She might not have taken the time to really look at who was standing beside her."

"You don't believe that," Isla said. There must have been some time they'd spent together. Surely Hendra had tried to sell the lie of the child's lineage to her wife. Or did she care too much to hide that from her—or not enough? Hendra wasn't someone Isla could get a handle on. But Alice, she had thought she understood. Isla had felt the hum and the healing within her. She hadn't been Rohen. She might have contained it, but she hadn't been a copy like they had left behind with Gray. "The woman I met was not Rohen," Isla said aloud, unsure why she needed to share that with him.

"You are sure?" he asked, something desperate in his voice.

She nodded once.

"Then we definitely need to go to Rennet to find out where she has gone and ensure the Hendra is not at risk."

"I've already told you, she is the safest woman in the universe."

He shook his head and moved his fingers through the controls. They were a long way from Rennet, and they would be alone together for some time yet.

Isla put her hand to the control panel in front of her and closed her eyes. The warm comfort of Rohen moved over her fingers. "Where is he?" she whispered.

"What are you playing at?" Calder asked, the harsh, cruel, familiar voice too near. She blinked into the light.

"I need to find Gray," she said.

He shook his head. "He isn't important in this."

"He is more than you think he is."

"To you maybe, but not to anyone else. I don't care if he is lying beneath tons of rock and forest." Isla sucked in a breath at the idea. "We are going to Hendra, and we are going to learn what that woman is."

Isla stood without acknowledging what he had said and moved back to the hard plastic seating behind the cockpit. She could leave him here alone, she thought as she strapped herself into the seat. She could find Gray and go. But she too needed to know what had happened to Alice and where she might be. And now that she understood what they had done with the asteroid, she needed to find the dust. Calder was the only way for her to do that.

Gray stood at the window wondering where in the universe Isla could be. His breath fogged up the glass as the sun started to rise over Oric, and he shivered. He had been standing so long at the window, watching the constant explosions around the city, that he hadn't realised just how cool it had become.

The Chief of Oric, Ebberah, had watched with him for hours and then disappeared. He couldn't remember if she'd spoken to him, said goodbye or taken off on some business or other. He stretched and rubbed at his eyes. He was tired, but he couldn't sleep. Too often he looked up at the ceiling to ensure it was still there.

"It is time," a quiet voice whispered as a warm hand found its way into his. He blinked at the reflection in the window and then down at the child beside him.

"Should we tell her we are going?" he asked, unsure why that was important. He didn't even know where they were going. In the ship, when Hari and the girl, Tevia, had saved him from the rubble, she had said someone wanted to see him. But he had ended up on Oric, again facing Ebberah who, despite being more than he had thought, had no idea what was really happening in the world. Even the uprising she thought she was behind worked separately from her, independent of her wishes, and it appeared Hari even thought her at risk from it.

"It is time," Tevia said again, her voice firm as though he were the child and didn't understand what was required of him.

He bowed his head to her and wondered what would be next as she led him towards the wall. Before he had the chance to consider what might happen, they were walking through a large, sparse room. The white walls appeared to glow with their own light, and then they were moving through another wall.

When he blinked into the dim light of the room, it was as though they had walked through a door rather than through two walls and he wasn't sure what else. He half expected to see the Readers of the moon of Oric again, but the room was small and cosy.

Dark green highlighted the wood panels, two armchairs sat in the middle of the space, bookshelves lined two of the walls and, as he turned slowly, taking in the lack of windows, a desk sat against a third wall. Someone sat at it hunched over something they were working on, and Tevia let go of his hand and disappeared.

Gray wasn't sure if he should cough or speak or give some indication he was there. He waited, wondering what he was doing, then stepped forward and peered over his shoulder. The desk was covered with sheets of paper, each bright white but rough around the edges. The figure was an older man who dipped a fine piece of wood in a jar and then scrawled something across the page. He moved it to the side and repeated the action. Gray focused on the writing and then stepped back. It was the odd characters they had seen at the lab, something he didn't understand to be anything other than a glitch in the system—and yet Isla had seen it as something else.

There was a knock at the door, and Gray took another step back. The man looked up, and a young man opened the door without waiting for an answer. "She's coming home," he said. The man nodded. The boy at the door looked up and locked eyes with Gray, but the older man shooed him away. As the door closed behind the young man, the older man turned to take in Gray.

"Sit down," he said, the words kind but firm. Gray bowed his head and sat in one of the soft chairs, sinking further than expected. "Thank you for coming."

"I wasn't sure I had the choice," Gray said.

The man smiled, made to lace his fingers and realised he still held the stick. He sat it on the desk and then tried again. He looked at Gray for some time as though trying to read him. Gray wondered if the man could read his mind. He rubbed at his eyes, finding they were getting heavy.

"You have come a long way."

"Where am I?" Gray asked, not sure he really wanted to know.

"Draroh."

Gray opened and then closed his mouth. Tevia certainly had a skill for moving through the Rohen, which confirmed for him that it was in fact everywhere and connected. No matter what Hendra thought she was doing.

"I am Minister Burre, advisor to the Chief of Draroh."

Gray bowed his head. "I am Gray E'anah. What are you writing?"

"Notes," the minister said with a wave of his hand as though they weren't important. Gray wondered then at the lack of technology in the room.

He glanced at the books, something that was talked of but that he hadn't seen since his days at school. He stood and took one from the shelf. The minister didn't seem to mind, watching as he carefully flipped through the pages. It seemed so delicate. But the text was not what he was expecting.

"What language is this?" he asked.

"Rohendra," the minister answered without hesitation.

"Why haven't I seen it before?"

"You likely have, at one time or another. You may not have appreciated what you were looking at."

"Can you teach me to read it?" Gray asked, a strange need filling him.

"Is that why you are here?"

"Why am I here?" he asked, trying to shake the feeling.

"So many reasons," the minister said. "The first of which is my daughter thinks you are important."

"Who is your daughter?" Gray asked, but he felt like he should know.

"She will be here soon enough to remind you," the minister said with a grin before the door opened again to a young woman.

"Father, would you like tea?"

He nodded, and she disappeared. Gray looked after her, but there was nothing familiar in the girl at all.

"I have several children," the minister said.

"Do you know where Isla is?" Gray asked. "Is she safe?"

"She is watched over. She had a task to complete..." His voice trailed off, and he rested his hand against the desk. "She has completed it, I hear."

"Who from?" Gray asked, sitting forward. The world was filled with too many questions. He didn't understand any of them, nor the answers, and it was becoming increasingly frustrating.

The older man smiled, and Gray wondered at the title. He appeared just as any older man. He didn't dress like he was in a position of power. In fact, Gray was sure he could see a hole worn through at one elbow.

"You are not as I imagined, either," the minister said kindly, a smile brightening his eyes. He waved towards the door as it opened, pushing into the room, and Gray wondered that he hadn't noticed it before. Why didn't it slide within the wall? The girl moved forward quickly with a tray and glanced at her father expectantly. With another wave of his hand, a table appeared for her to set the tray down. Gray was certain that Reilly would have called that magic if he had been here to see it.

The girl poured tea into two cups and handed one to him, then one to her father. He waved his hand again and she scurried out the door, closing it behind her.

"Why is there no technology?" Gray asked, although he wondered if that were true, looking at the table that had appeared from nothing.

"It is not needed," the older man said. "Biscuit?"

Gray looked to the plate of biscuits in the centre of the tray. Had he not been paying attention or had these just been magicked up? It had been some time since he had eaten, but he was sure he could still taste the dust of the facility that had fallen around him. He shook his head.

"Try the tea. It will help."

Gray sipped at it slowly and was reminded of the tea Alice had fed him when he had been shot. "She's missing," he murmured and took another sip.

"I have a good idea where she is."

"Do you know that the Hendra is searching for her?"

"She has her ideas," the minister said, taking a sip of his tea.

"Ideas you have provided."

The old man looked up from his cup and smiled. "I like you, and I think we are going to be firm friends."

"Why did you want to see me?" Gray asked again.

"Oh, so many reasons." The man leaned forward, took a biscuit from the tray and popped it into his mouth.

Two

Hendra sat on the floor against the glass looking out over the city that stretched out from her office. There had been some vibrations during the night, but it was calm now. The Elite and the enforcers had been sent out at the first signs of trouble and continued to move through the streets. The trouble seemed to have sprung up around the Complex with little warning.

She watched the sun glinting off the buildings, wondering at how beautiful it was. Had she not really taken the time to look before? Had she not taken the time to listen? There must have been warning—there must have been some hint of what was going on. The whole universe hadn't suddenly risen up together in a wave overnight.

The door opened, and the general appeared. He rushed forward and knelt over her. "Have you been here all night?" he asked, putting the back of his hand to her cheek. When had these men decided she was someone they could handle?

She nodded slowly and turned back to the view. It didn't really matter anymore. Then the general was lifting her away from the cold comfort of the glass, holding her against his chest and moving out through the building with her in his arms.

"This is not necessary," she murmured, resting too easily against his chest.

"I want the doctor to look you over. Calder is returning, and he would be stern with me if I didn't do all that I could."

"Calder is returning," she repeated.

"He wants to look at Alice," he murmured.

"You told him?" she asked, finding she had more strength than she realised.

"Asking for anything to be kept quiet involves Colonel Calder. He is singularly in charge of your protection."

"He'll bring the girl with him," she muttered.

"Likely. Although I'm not sure what he gets from that."

"Did she find what she wanted?"

"I don't know. You can ask yourself, once the doctor has looked you over." He was sitting her down on the bed in a room Hendra had thought she would never have to revisit.

The doctor was already waiting, and he began moving a wand over her body before the general had even stepped back. He pulled a pad from his pocket, but Hendra shook her head. The man waved an arm, and the image appeared before her.

There were no fuzzy lights, no strange writing along the base of the screen. It appeared just as her last one. Although the child looked somewhat more defined, perhaps.

"You need rest and nourishment. I suggest a good meal and a good night's sleep."

She sighed.

"You are responsible for more than yourself," the doctor chastised.

"I have been responsible for more than myself for the whole of my life," she said. "That won't change given that I am with child. My great grandmother delivered her first child at her desk in the middle of a council meeting."

The doctor laughed, and Hendra was momentarily taken aback by the sound. "That does not mean it is ideal. At your age, and after such an illness, if you want this child to succeed you, you must look after the two of you."

She looked down at her lap. He was right. And Alice was no longer here to ensure that she did look after them—nor, it appeared, had she been here from the time the child was conceived. Or perhaps she had been around then... Hendra had no idea. She looked at the general.

"I'll call your staff," he muttered, but she reached for him as he made to leave the room.

"You may leave us," she said to the doctor, who bowed his head and left. "I need to know when she died."

"We are working on it, but it is hard to determine. After such a period, the body has..."

She waved her hand to indicate he should go on, that it wasn't difficult for her to hear, although it was much harder than she'd imagined. It was the reason she had told Alice the truth about the child's origins, almost. The information, at least, that the child wasn't a part of them. But then she hadn't been telling Alice that, even if she'd thought she had.

"I can't do this." At the slight rise of the general's eyebrows, she realised she had said it aloud. She took a deep breath, nodded slowly and allowed him to help her to her feet.

She had been transported to her own apartment, which felt empty and cold despite the number of staff standing around the table watching her eat. The general was one of them. She had tried to get him to sit down and eat with her, but he was having none of it. And so she was eating alone, surrounded by many. As soon as she laid the fork down, the general stepped forward and assisted her from the chair.

"Are you going to escort me to my room as well?" she asked, trying to indicate just how annoyed she was with him. But when he nodded once, she was relieved. She was almost tempted to ask him to come inside, but when he left her at the door, she was thankful to have some space to herself. Although, the bed did appear very large and lonely.

She sat on the edge of it and kicked off her shoes. She lay down, curled into a ball and focused on what she would do if she ever came across the woman pretending to be Alice.

Alice hadn't been very close to her of late. She had sat in her lap not long ago, but that had ended all too quickly. Besides that, she would either be asleep when Hendra did come to bed or sleeping when she woke. They would eat together, talk together—and yet Hendra suddenly wondered if she had truly known the woman. But was it Alice? Had this started when she'd learnt of the child, or before? She couldn't remember, and she chastised herself for her lack of attention.

But she had so much to pay attention to. She was responsible for the whole of the solar system, so many lives, so many activities, and one woman could slip through the cracks. Slip from the list of what was important to pay attention to.

"I'm sorry," Hendra murmured, rolling onto her back and looking up at the ceiling. "You should have been the most important thing in my life. I should have paid you more attention."

She should have looked after Alice better, she thought, thinking of the body lying for so long undetected. Had she been alone when she died? Scared? No matter what she tried, the memories of their conversations, dinners, the brief moments wrapped in each other's arms in this very bed, she could not determine when her wife had gone and another had taken her place.

She shook her head, closed her eyes and tried to halt the hot tears that flowed too freely. She rolled over into a ball again, pulled the pillow in close and sobbed freely, for a love she had lost, a woman she hadn't treated as she should have, and her own failing.

Hendra woke to the sound of voices and wondered if she had slept long. As the voices increased in volume and intensity, she sat up, ran her fingers through her hair, wiped at her face and hoped she looked better than she felt. She opened the door to the general's back and Calder growling some threat.

"I'm awake," she said.

The general turned apologetic eyes her way while Calder pushed the man out of the way and into the room.

"Tell me," he said, looking her over with his hands on her shoulders.

She shrugged out of his hold and looked around him to see if he had brought the girl with him to her bedroom door.

"What do you know?" Calder asked, drawing her attention.

"Nothing," she said, turning back to him. "Nothing other than she is gone." She was surprised she had managed to keep her voice level.

"Would you like breakfast, Your Grace?" someone asked from the doorway.

"I just had breakfast," Hendra murmured, but her stomach growled.

"Yesterday," the general whispered.

"I must have needed the sleep," she returned, although she wondered if she had slept at all. She was sure that she had spent much of the time in the dimly lit room, staring at the ceiling and trying to remember what she couldn't. "I would rather we take this discussion to the dining room," she said, heading out into the hallway. She was surprised when Calder took her arm and stopped her, pulling her close.

She put her hand on his chest and shook her head. "I don't need your comfort. I need your skills," she said, her voice firm. She was sure she staggered as she went out into the hallway to find the general, several members of staff and the hummer. She glared at the girl, who bowed her head.

"Prepare my clothes," she said to one of the staff. "And breakfast," she muttered to someone else. "The rest of you may leave me to get ready for the day, and we will start again in the dining room."

"Yes, Your Grace," was the chorused reply.

She waited for Calder to leave her room and then followed the staff back in, pushed the door closed and leaned against it. Whether she was ready or not, she would have to face the day.

Calder stared through the glass, and Isla wondered how in the universe they were so certain that the remains spread out on the table on the other side could be Alice.

"You would know," Calder whispered. She blinked at him, wondering if he had read her mind in some way.

"Excuse me?"

"You met with her, hid with her." His voice was harsh as he turned slowly, and she was tempted to take a step back. "You would have known if the woman was something else."

"If she was Rohen?" Isla asked, looking back at the dark, charred flesh. As a soldier, she had seen worse—she might have looked much like this herself when they had dragged her from the battlefield or forest that day. She shook her head. Whatever Alice might have been, or her imposter, it was not Rohen. There was skill there, a connection to the Rohen, and the moments she had thought the woman had disappeared seemed to make more sense.

"Is she a hummer?" Calder asked.

Isla shook her head again. Watching the man leaning over the remains, his mask pulled tight and a clear shield covering his entire face, the pale green scrubs smudged with gore reminded Isla suddenly of the room she had been in with Alice. He didn't once glance up at them, and she wondered how long he had been working on the body. It had been found days ago, or so she had thought.

"Come on," Calder muttered. She turned from the window to find him making his way towards the door. Before she could suggest this was a bad idea, he was in the room. The man continued to work, poking through the body, taking samples. How many samples would they need to ensure she was dead? Or to determine when it had happened?

"How long?" Calder asked.

"I am trying to work that out," the man said.

"Work faster," Calder growled.

The man sighed, but did not look up. Something pulled at Isla, something uncomfortable.

"Why don't they want us to know?" she asked. The man looked up for the first time, blinking slowly. She wondered then, as the light appeared to catch the silver threads in his eyes, if that was the reflection from his mask.

"Who?" he asked. But she knew he was well aware of what she meant.

"Why wouldn't they want us to know?" Calder asked, his attention on her rather than the short man.

"I don't..." But did she know the answer to that already? If they couldn't tell when Alice had died, they might not be able to truly trace what had happened to her, when things had changed, who had been responsible. Isla studied the man openly staring at her now. Had the Rohen done this? Or was it something else?

Isla stepped forward and studied the mess before her. It could have been anyone. "How did you know it was her?" she asked.

The man made a noise as though she had no understanding of the world.

"How?" she asked again.

"There are many tests, simple ones to determine such things."

"And yet you can't determine when she died," Calder commented.

"Show me," Isla demanded.

"I don't think..."

"The Hendra herself has sent us," Calder replied, his voice lifting even the hairs on the back of Isla's neck.

The man audibly gulped. Then he pulled a wand from the panel on the wall and ran it over the remains. He pressed some buttons, and a monitor above them flickered to life with Alice's smiling face looking back at them.

"Hmmm," Calder murmured from the end of the platform.

"So the material is not degraded far enough not to identify that."

"No," the man said simply, his eyes shining.

"Run the tests," Isla said.

He shook his head. Calder growled, but Isla was already on her way out of the room and tugging Calder along with her.

"He knows more than he is saying," Calder muttered once they were back in the hall. The man watched them as they walked past the window.

"It isn't her," Isla whispered.

"What?" Calder pulled her to a stop, his hand too tight around her arm.

"It isn't her," she repeated.

"You saw the same image I did."

"It was a plant. If they had enough material to find that information, then they could have determined when she died just as easily. The secret here is not when but who."

"You aren't making sense."

"I don't know what Alice is," Isla said, turning back for the door. "But she isn't dead."

Gray pulled another volume from the bookcase, surprised by the weight of the book in his hands and tempted to smell the pages. There was something both foreign and comforting in the scent. The minister had assured him he would learn the words, that the understanding was in him somewhere already, but no matter what he glanced through or tried to study, the images and text made no more sense to him than when he had thought them a glitch in the lab.

He sighed and closed the volume in his hand. He slotted it back into the gap between the others he had taken it from when a hand reached past him, took it back and the placed it elsewhere on the shelf.

He tried not to stare at the woman beside him. "Where did you come from?" he asked.

"Rennet," she said, not looking at him, her eyes running over the books. "Did you put them back in this haphazard manner?"

"I put them back where I pulled them from."

"Are you sure?" Alice asked, turning to him. Her eyes sparkled as she smiled.

He bowed his head to her, suddenly aware of how close he stood, and stepped back. "They are looking for you," he murmured.

"Not as you would think," she said, turning back to the shelves.

He waited as she continued to search the shelves in silence and then reached for a book. The movement lengthened her body, and he noticed how young and agile she appeared. Had he realised that before? Wasn't the Hendra so much older?

She turned a grin on him as though she had read his thoughts. He stepped back and sat down. She handed him the book, which he took without looking at it. She looked at it pointedly and then to him.

"I can't read it." He said it as though it were a sign of weakness. When had this language last been spoken or written in the Complex?

"Yes, you can," she said, sitting on the small table before his chair.

He shook his head.

"You can," she said more forcefully, putting her hand on his knee. Although it was warm and comforting, even through the thick material of his trousers, he flinched. "Go on," she said as though he hadn't moved.

He opened the book and looked over the text. "This is common," he muttered.

She shook her head. Her soft blonde hair swayed with the movement, and he was momentarily captivated.

"Rohendra," he murmured.

She bowed her head, her hand pressing a little harder on his leg. He looked back at the page and wondered why it suddenly made sense. The words leapt out at him, the image they evoked appearing like a monitor and rising from the paper. Men and fear.

"They hid," he whispered.

She bowed her head and lifted her hand.

"They shouldn't have hidden," he murmured.

"There was no option other than to fight. They hoped for something better."

"But it didn't happen."

"No," she said, standing. She looked and sounded sad.

"Why did you run away, Alice?" he asked, closing the book and standing.

"I have done as I was instructed."

"And what was that?"

She smiled again, still sad. "Finding a way to heal the rift."

"Heal it?" he asked. "The queen?"

She smiled and ran her fingers over his cheek. In many ways, she reminded him of Tevia, and yet she was so different. So clean.

"Has Isla done as she was asked?" he questioned, unsure why he knew Alice would hold the answers.

She bowed her head and removed her fingers.

"The uprising, the fighting."

"They will come to understand," she said, turning for the door.

"Wait!" he called after her. "Are you a hummer?"

She stopped with her hand on the door and tilted her head a little to the side. He wondered if she was listening to something else, the Rohen perhaps, as Tevia had done. A conversation he wasn't a part of.

She turned back to him standing in the small room, the book in his hand, and with a sigh she indicated the chair. He sat back down. She sat beside him but didn't say anything.

"You healed my leg," he said, tapping his knee. There wasn't even a mark. "Do you have a way with creams like Isla?"

"It is a little different, my skill and hers."

"But you hum?"

"That seems a strange term. I wonder where it started," she murmured, looking back over the bookcase.

"I'm sure the answer is in there somewhere," he said. "What would you call it?"

"Talking." She shrugged, then sighed and looked at him seriously. "There is a hum to the universe," she said as though she didn't really want to tell him anything. "That hum is..." She waved her hand.

"The heart of the universe," he whispered. Had he heard Isla say that very thing, or was it something else—or someone else?

She nodded, and her smile made him sit back a little more in the comfortable chair and relax. "The hum is the heartbeat. It is the Rohen. The Rohendra," she said. "Some of us can feel it more acutely than others. It may be that those trying to explain their sense of the world described it as a hum and became known as hummers."

"Why were they seen as dangerous?"

"They weren't—not by all. Isla's people understood what she was, what she would become. The people of the forests of Draroh also understand."

"The fear of the unknown. Is that why Hendra is so determined to destroy them?"

"She is selfish and does not want to share power."

"Does she know just what she fights?"

"No," Alice said, standing up again and brushing out the non-existent creases of her skirt. "She will come to understand."

"Do they want to work with her, or replace her?"

Alice, the First Wife of the Rohendra Complex, smiled, bowed her head and left the room. Gray watched the door long after she was gone and wondered if Isla would find him here. Did she know where he was? Had she finished with her task? She might believe him under the rubble of the facility on Oric. But then she wouldn't have left him there. He hoped.

He looked back over the bookcase and the book in his hand, sat back and opened it again. He would read and learn all he could of the history of the connection with these people and find a way he could help.

Three

Hendra felt as though she could breathe for the first time in too long as Calder marched into her office. She tried to make a show of looking away from the reports she was reading, but she had looked for him every time the door opened. She stood slowly at the desk, brushing her fingers over the control to make the monitors disappear. She stepped out from behind the desk as the hummer followed him through the door.

She thought he would offer some further comfort, or condolence, but he stood at attention too far away from her.

"What took you so long to respond to my request?" she asked, amazed that her voice remained level.

"I was busy." He glanced over his shoulder, but the woman behind him was focused on Hendra rather than him, as though she was trying to read her.

"Not a good enough excuse. You are busy with what I tell you to be busy with. Alice..." she started.

Fearing the threatening tears, she moved quickly towards the table and indicated he take a seat. The last time they had sat here together, he had fed her steak. He did at least pull a chair out for her at the head of the table. Island waited behind a chair as she sat, and then they sat opposite each other, one on either side. She wondered what they were planning, for they were clearly working together. That wasn't what she had intended when she'd sent Calder after the hummer.

Island opened her mouth, sighed something and then looked to Calder.

"You have seen her," Hendra said. That was why he had come, after all—to ensure Alice was dead, and the traitor he had claimed her to be. Although that didn't seem to matter now.

"Your man in the morgue can't be trusted," he said, his voice low and stern.

"The general vouches for him."

"Then perhaps the general cannot be trusted either," he said, leaning forward.

"What is it?' she asked, leaning towards him as though they were the only two in the whole world.

He stammered then, as though unsure what to tell her.

"I need to know when she died."

"The woman on the slab?" the hummer asked. "We would need another pathologist."

"Surely we have the technology to learn this. Why is it taking so long?" Hendra asked Calder, ignoring the woman.

"The man won't say," Calder said. "We believe"—he glanced across at the woman opposite—"that the woman, the body that they have is not Alice."

"Not Alice," Hendra breathed, wiping at her face. Could that be possible? Could Alice still be alive? "They assured me it was her."

Isla shook her head. "They lied. Although we aren't sure who is behind the lie or why."

"Of course we are," Hendra snapped, looking to Calder.

"I can't understand why the Rohen would do this," Island continued.

"You know them so well?" Hendra spat.

Island shook her head. "They have their reasons; they have their ways. I can't see the benefit in this, other than to allow Alice an escape. For you to believe that the woman who has been changing you was the woman you trusted."

Hendra sat back and studied the young woman. What did she know? What would she really tell her?

"It was poison," Calder growled, and Isla shook her head.

"What exactly do you think they were doing to me? That Alice was doing? Whatever it was has failed. The infection or poison has cleared my system. The child is fine."

The girl smiled then, a genuine but knowing smile. "The child was never in doubt, Your Grace."

Hendra looked down slowly, her hand resting on her belly. A small wave of movement rippled over the skin beneath her fingers.

"What have they done?"

"Nothing," Island said, her voice certain, and yet Hendra suddenly felt more devastated than she had at the news of Alice's death.

"What is it that the two of you have learnt that you are not sharing with me?" she asked, trying to sound as though it didn't affect her as much as it did. Her heart was racing, her mind spinning. What were they to each other that they would hide from her, that Calder would hold back?

"I am not hiding anything," he murmured. She shook her head to dispel the strange thoughts bubbling away. He growled something under his breath and stood.

The hummer looked at her with more feeling than Hendra thought the girl had, or that she wanted shown towards her. She didn't need this girl's pity. She was the leader of the Rohendra Complex, and she would remain so no matter what any random group thought they could do with demonstrations and bombings—nor what the Rohen themselves thought they could do to her. She noticed then that her hands hadn't left her belly, but she couldn't seem to lift them away.

"Your child..." the hummer said, leaning in closer, her voice soft and soothing as though she were talking to a child. Hendra riled at the idea of it.

"What of my child?" she interrupted.

"Your child is very important to the Rohendra. They would not harm it."

"It, as you so insensitively put it, is the next leader of this solar system."

The girl nodded and leaned back. Just what did she think she had learnt while she was out there?

"The Rohen do not want to work with us," Hendra snapped.

"The Rohendra," Island said, using that word again—the word her father had used, "has worked with us for longer than any of us realise or understand. Why would you want to change things?"

"I'm not changing anything, and how would you know they worked with us?"

"The trouble started when you tried to remove them," Calder said, leaning on the back of the chair he stood behind.

"You were involved with that operation yourself," she muttered. "You both were," she said more clearly as she looked at Island Tarle, the only one to survive.

"You sent us in. You are trying to contain them now that you cannot remove them from the Complex. If you were to work with them as your father did, then the trouble would stop."

"And if I don't?" she asked, the defiance clear in her voice. She was the leader of this universe; she would not be dictated to by a girl.

"Then they will work with your child," Island said, pushing her seat back and looking at Calder as she stood.

"Where is Alice?" Hendra asked, looking between the two of them.

The girl shrugged.

"I don't know," Calder muttered.

"I want her found." Hendra looked between the two of them again.

"It isn't important," Isla said, walking towards the door.

"Then why bother telling me that she is still out there and responsible for what happened to me?"

"You already knew she was responsible," Island said without turning back.

"Stop her!" Hendra screamed at Calder, who too calmly watched her walk away.

"We have done as we were asked."

"You have done hardly anything I have asked of you of late. And her task was to talk to the Rohen, get it to do as I wanted it to."

"It is not possible," Island said, her hand on the door.

Hendra stood as the girl left the office without waiting to be dismissed. Had no one any respect anymore? Calder followed her out. Was he chasing her down or following? Hendra wondered as she watched the door for too long with neither of them returning.

Gray walked back and forth across the small office, the book in his hand so absorbing of his attention that he fell over the small table. It was only as he then made himself comfortable on the floor that he realised there was someone else in the room. He looked up at Alice smiling down on him.

"You did this," he murmured, finding it hard to look away from the pages. He had only read as he needed to as a child and during his time as an enforcer, and only news flashes since then. Now he had to know—had to devour everything about the Rohen while he could. It was almost as though he was overwhelmed by the fear that if he stopped, his ability to read the words would disappear, or the books themselves would disappear, and he would never learn all that was contained within them.

"You need to eat," Alice chided as though he were a child.

"Where have you been?" he asked, wondering just how long he had sat or walked with a book in his hand in this very room. When was the last time he had left? His stomach growled, and he reluctantly sat the book down on the table. He wanted to put the pages down so he would know where he was, but he closed it. He looked about for something to mark his spot but feared what it might do to the pages or the delicate ink.

"Gray. Eat. The books will not disappear. I had a similar moment as a child, when the words first made sense and leapt from the page. But they will remain."

"How long ago were you a child?" he asked without thinking, and she smiled but shook her head.

"Sorry," he murmured.

"I am probably younger than you." Laughter tinged her words, and he wasn't sure if she was laughing at him or at the idea of him thinking her older. Hendra was certainly older. He pressed his lips closed. "I did as I was instructed."

He nodded then, understanding exactly what she meant. Although he hadn't been instructed to do anything, he knew what the images from the books led to. He understood what Isla felt with the Rohen even though he couldn't experience any of it; or at least he hadn't yet. He wondered if he would. If he could feel what she felt. Reading the pages gave him hope.

"You are lost," she whispered, sitting down on the floor beside him and moving the book further out of his reach.

"I feel found," he murmured, reaching past her. She pushed it behind her, further from his reach, and leaned in towards him at the same time.

He leaned towards her. Like the books, she drew him in. He paused, and as she leaned closer, he leaned back. "I can feel you hum," he murmured.

"Can you?" she asked, leaning in again, and he was on his feet and stepping away. "Not many can feel that who are not hummers. There is something about you, something they have chosen—that is why you can read the texts."

"I can talk to Rohen," he murmured, remembering boasting to Isla about such a thing. Although he knew it to be true, it didn't seem like something he needed to tell her.

She tilted her head a little and studied him. He felt uncomfortable for the first time, unsure of this woman. He wondered if she really was a woman, if she really was the woman he thought she was.

"Did you tell Hendra we were there?" he asked, and she was shaking her head before he had finished asking the question.

"She had me watched more closely than I realised," Alice said softly. "I thought I could help."

"Did she not trust you? Was there a reason not to trust you?" he asked, looking over the books.

"I was there for a reason, to help her become what she needed to be. Hendra does not trust anyone. The only one she truly trusted was her father, and in his dying breath he told her a truth she couldn't believe. It sent her on an unexpected path."

"Who sent you in?"

Alice raised her eyebrows, and he wasn't sure if she didn't understand or if she was amazed that he would ask.

"Why was her path unexpected?"

"It was thought she was something else. Destined to be something else."

"And her child will be instead."

Alice nodded, stood slowly and motioned him towards the door. "Come and eat."

She waited on the other side of the door for him, then took his arm and walked along the corridor into a dining room. It was a cosy space, and yet larger than the office he had spent so much time in. One wall was floor-to-ceiling windows that looked out into a dense forest of trees. Children ran around the table and over chairs, and one dived under the table. Gray sat where Alice indicated as the minister entered the room. The rabble eased, and everyone sat down.

As Gray sat the book on the table beside him, he realised it had been harder to leave the learning behind. A girl across the table, no more than ten summers, laughed.

"He is just like you," she said, looking at Alice. "It calls him."

He studied the book and then the child as Alice heaped food from a dish onto his plate. He glanced around at the others helping themselves, some of the children standing on chairs to lean over the table and taking heaped spoonfuls of what they wanted. The majority of dishes appeared to be vegetable based, nearly all of them cooked in ways Gray wasn't familiar with. Although it smelt great, he longed for some meat.

"What calls?" he asked, pushing his fork reluctantly into something orange, not quite sure he wanted to taste it.

"Vegetables are good for you," Alice chided, and the girl grinned.

"The Rohendra," she said.

He stared at her for a moment.

"The boy is just learning," the minister said from the head of the table. "Leave him."

The girl sat back, tucked her blonde hair behind her ears and focused on her food.

Gray started to eat. There were so many questions he wanted to ask, but he had no idea where to start. Just what connection did these people have to the Rohen that the children talked of them openly? As he looked across at the girl eating, he noticed the small tendrils of silver moving from her fingers and occasionally through her hair. He blinked at the silence that seemed to have descended on the room, glancing at Alice and then the minister.

"We need to give him some time," the minister said.

The girl nodded. The tendrils disappeared, and the noise started again amongst the children. When Gray looked again at Alice, she was looking at her plate. She gave a subtle shake of her head, and he rested his hand on the book beside him. The girl opposite him giggled.

"Beth," the minister warned.

"Yes, Father," she said, and she bowed her head at Gray.

"Who else here knows the secrets?" Gray asked.

"It isn't a secret," Beth said, her face scrunching as though she didn't understand the question.

"Not you," Gray said, raising his hand to indicate the child before pulling it back to the book. "The Rohen."

"The Rohendra are not a secret," the child answered, and Alice cleared her throat. "Not here." She looked at Alice with the same confusion on her face, as though he was talking of something she really didn't understand.

"You are all hummers," Gray said. The minister sighed and put down his utensils as Alice rested a hand on his arm.

"We don't really use that term here," he said as though he had explained it a thousand times before. "We, they"—he swept his hand, indicating the children around the table—"are connected to the heartbeat of the universe. As are we all in some way," he added, looking pointedly at Gray.

Gray looked at the book beneath his fingers, the words within calling to him.

"We are as we are. Not all in the Complex understand that or would be willing to accept the state of things as they truly are. This is the way. This has always been the way, only not everyone knows that."

Gray nodded as a sign of understanding, yet he didn't fully understand what was happening around him. "The demonstrations, the attacks, they were the Rohen... Rohendra?"

Beth cocked her head to the side as she studied him across the table.

"We will talk, but it isn't as you imagine it to be. Eat and then we will show you our world."

He bowed his head again and turned back to his plate. He realised then that Alice's hand was still on his arm. He glanced at her, but she kept it there, and he wasn't sure if it was for support or if she was reading him in some way. Or was she giving him something else, like the ability to read the books?

Four

Isla walked around the office in Hendra Central with some level of surprise that she had made it back here and at the images and awards that covered the wall opposite Calder's desk. She also contained a certain level of wariness that he might at any stage lock her away again, whether in a glass cell or elsewhere.

The world hummed around her. Despite Hendra's knowledge of what they needed to contain the Rohen, there wasn't anything in place to keep it from Hendra Central.

"Does she want to change the world we know?" Isla asked, studying an image of a group of soldiers, none of which she recognised. She wondered again if anyone knew who he had been and why no one had questioned where he had come from. "Did you just appear after that day and...?" She couldn't even guess at how it had been done.

"I transferred into a new unit; no one questioned where I came from. I was experienced, and I got things done."

"The Sparrow," she murmured, looking over another image. They could have been her team, those she'd worked with all those years ago, but again the faces were unfamiliar.

"There were others," he said.

She turned and took him in as he sat straight behind the desk looking like a soldier, and yet he seemed so far from it. He did as he was directed, or at least he had. Now he was thinking for himself. "You didn't answer the question," she prompted.

"She wants to control it."

"She already does," Isla said, turning back to the wall and reviewing more images just the same. In one, he appeared much younger than he was, as though he would have been in this group before she knew him, but he had Calder's face and not Kalli's. She put her finger to the image, and he sighed.

"She doesn't control all of it," he said. "We had to make it look like I was who she said I was."

"Why did you do this?" Isla asked. "I don't even want to know why you would have sacrificed us—but why become this?" She indicated his body with her hands.

"It isn't all that bad," he said, grinning at her in a way that made her shiver. It was a smile he might have given her so long ago, but it scared her now.

"I want to say that it isn't who you were, but then you were never who I thought..." She shook her head, chasing the memories away. The man before her stood slowly and came around the desk. There was something in the way he moved, something familiar in him, and she backed up. His expression changed, the soft welcoming face suddenly becoming the face that scared her.

"Once," he murmured.

"He's gone," she said.

"And now there is the enforcer."

She didn't have to explain any of this to him. Not what Gray was to her, as she didn't really know, nor what her feelings might be for anything. He had no right to any information about her.

"Why does she need to control the Rohen? She can still run the Complex, can still function as she always has."

"It isn't who she is," he said with a slight shrug of one shoulder.

"There is more between you than there should be," Isla said, and the hard eyes turned her way again. "Even though you are helping me and not doing as she has directed."

"And what am I helping you with?" he asked, looking away. She felt relief from his lack of attention. "You wanted to know how it was contained. Now you know. I'm not helping you. I'm helping the Complex by getting you to do what we need."

"I can't do what you need. I'm helping someone else."

"Gray," he murmured.

"Rohendra," she replied. "And although we know what the containment is, you haven't shown me where it is."

"I don't know." He looked up then, as though it had never occurred to him that he wouldn't know it all.

"Can you find out?"

He raised a monitor she could only see the hum of from her position on the other side of his desk, his eyes glazing as he scanned something. She watched him for a while, and then he put his hand to the comm panel and paused. His eyes met hers for the first time as he waved her from the room. She smiled at the idea that he thought he was keeping things from her. She didn't think it would take too long to learn how he came across the information or whom he talked to—she just needed to know where it was.

She left the office, pausing outside the door, and wasn't surprised that she couldn't hear anything on the other side. There was no one in the corridor. She walked away, wondering how much freedom she really had in the building. If she was seen to be working with Hendra and Calder, then anyone she came across might not question her presence.

She wandered aimlessly for some time, running her fingers along the walls and listening to the heartbeat, the hum, of the Rohen. She wondered again how they needed her to find what they would surely understand far better.

She closed her eyes and followed the hum, the pull towards she wasn't sure what. A couple of times she heard something, a mutter or the sounds of boots trying to get out of the way. But she maintained her slow walk, letting the Rohen guide her through the building. When she stopped, she was standing in an office that appeared somewhat different to the other rooms at Central. She glanced back out into the hallway, but there was no one there, and she had no idea where she was in relation to Calder's office.

She looked back into the room. A desk sat in the middle, a simple chair behind it. She ran her hand over the wood, feeling the Rohen buzz and hum beneath her fingers as she sensed the forest, and the smell of the trees.

She sat slowly in the chair and ran her fingers across the wood when a monitor hummed to life before her. Words flowed across the screen, letters, symbols and characters she couldn't understand.

"What are you trying to tell me?" she whispered.

She blinked several times, and the words came into focus, the letters making sense suddenly. She leaned back, and then it was gone. The odd-shaped symbols returned, and she squinted at them, but couldn't understand.

Isla looked up at the stark walls, crisp and clean and perfectly clear. She stood from the desk, and the monitor disappeared. She moved to the nearest wall and ran her fingers over the cool white surface. Small tendrils of Rohen reached out to meet her as they had when she had shown her skills to the Chief of Oric. They pulled at her, called to her, and she was tempted to let them carry her away. She had found what they had wanted, although she was yet to find where it was stored. She had completed her task. She needed another, needed something to occupy her or she was lost. She longed for Gray, and an image filled her mind of him surrounded by children. She smiled at the idea, but she didn't know if it was his location or just an idea of him. He looked just the same, although perhaps tired. Was the Rohen pulling at him again, making him unwell?

"We didn't do that," a voice whispered in her mind.

"Help me?" she asked, uncertain what she needed help with. She was meant to be helping them. She was always sure she had to help the Rohen. Was she asked—was she pleading? She had learnt more of who she was and yet was surrounded by uncertainty.

"You are..."

The door banged open. Calder stood in the doorway, his features angry, and the Rohen around her fingers disappeared, lost to her. Although she could feel it close, it pulled away. She looked at the man in the doorway, wondering again if they were pulling away from him.

"You are determined to separate them. There is a fear," she murmured.

"I am not afraid of them," he growled.

"You saw them, that day."

He shook his head, but she saw it in his face. The fear, the horror.

"You saw them," she repeated, her voice low. As she stepped towards him, he stepped away. "What did you see?" she asked, needing to know more of what had happened that day. She didn't feel the same fear as when she'd learnt who they were and what they had done to her. It was the uncertainty, the not knowing that made it hard for her.

He shook his head. "I found the dust."

"Dust?" she asked.

"The meteors."

She nodded, wanting to reach out for the wall, to have the Rohen show her what he was and what he knew. There was more to this man, more than she understood. They were sure he would help her, and she couldn't understand why that would be.

"You want to see it, don't you?" he asked, almost taunting, as though he knew where it was but wasn't going to share that information with her.

She bowed her head, clenching her hands to stop herself from reaching out.

"What will you do then?"

"I don't know," she said. "I just know I have to see it."

He turned as though the conversation she was trying to have hadn't just happened. She waited a moment longer in the office before she followed him out.

"Why there?" he asked when she'd caught up to him.

"Sorry?"

"Why that office?"

"Just looking, just wandering, and then I found myself there."

"It doesn't work."

"Excuse me?" She followed him around a corner and found she was working hard to keep up with him, both with the conversation and the speed at which he was walking. They passed other soldiers who stopped and saluted, which he returned and she ignored. Their eyes followed her, but no one said anything. It wouldn't take long for word of her being in the building to spread.

"The office you were in," he said, suddenly stopping. "It doesn't work. Some issue we could never work out, and so it isn't used unless someone wants a quiet space to talk. No matter what we do as soldiers, we need the communication and monitors."

"The monitor worked," Isla said, and he looked back down the corridor. "The wood was different," she added. Maybe they had been waiting for someone else—maybe there were far more hummers in the world than she had realised or taken the time to consider. She had asked the question, hadn't she?

He shook his head slowly.

"Where is the dust?" she asked. She refocused on where they were, and then they were in a lift heading out across the foyer into the sun and bright buildings of Rennet. He had not spoken or looked at her in that time.

She wondered if she would ever know what he was thinking or planning. "Rennet?" she asked. He nodded once and continued down the street.

Several people paused and watched them walk by, but no one spoke to them. No one approached. Isla saw an enforcer step towards them, recognise Calder and appear to think better of it.

A sleek black vehicle pulled up beside them. The door opened, and Calder stepped into it without hesitation. Isla looked for too long before joining him. The interior of the vehicle was dark, and it was moving before she fully found her seat, slipping to the side and against Calder.

He muttered something as he helped her into a seat. Soft blue light illuminated the space, which was much larger than she had imagined it to be. It was odd that she had wondered about the vehicles but never been in one. Even as a reported war hero being ferried between Central and the hearings, she wasn't that lucky.

She gulped as she noticed Calder watching her with the same look he'd had in his office, the one that made her nervous because it reminded her so much of Kalli.

"You haven't told me where we are going," she said.

"I don't want you to know," he said, looking away for the first time. "You want to see the dust. I am willing to show you that, but I'm not willing to share with you what you will use against us."

"I thought you wanted to help. That is what I am trying to do."

"No, you are trying to let the Rohen take what they want rather than give us what we need."

"They give you what you need—all the time—and yet you want to prevent that. Hendra is creating a divide that will not end in your favour. You are helping with that. They don't like it and they won't support it."

"But they are happy enough for you to come with me?"

Isla sighed. "They are sure you will help. I'm not so sure you will."

"But you trust them."

She nodded. There were times she had feared them. Even now, there were times she was somewhat nervous of what they were or what they could do. That they were willing to risk the people of the Complex in a revolution to get them what they needed in the end. They needed the Hendra's child, who wouldn't become the leader they needed anytime soon.

"What is the news on the fighting?"

"Sporadic. It appears to have eased for the moment, and there is no sign of who the ringleaders are or how we might find them."

"I don't think you can," Isla murmured. She couldn't tell from the movement of the vehicle the direction they travelled or if they had even moved from where they were collected, only the hum of the engine. They sat in continued silence, and she wondered just why he was here. Did Calder really think he was helping the Hendra by allowing her what she thought she needed? Although Isla was sure he wasn't doing that—he was after something else.

The vehicle slowed, and Isla pressed her hand into the soft material of the seat beside her. The threads of Rohen called but didn't reach out to her, and then they were gone. She pushed ahead of Calder as the door opened and stepped out into a dimly lit warehouse to instant disappointment.

There was nothing there. No one to greet them—no one to explain any of it. Dust covered the floor and, as Isla stepped away from him, the empty echo and lack of Rohen hurt her as it had in the facility on Oric.

Five

G ray followed the girl down the hallway and out into the forest. He stopped, looking into the green light that filtered through the trees. The expanse of forest before him was enormous, and he couldn't remember moving through the trees to get here in the first place. Or had he? No, he had been moved straight to the minister's library. Although what his role was exactly, Gray wasn't sure.

Despite the size of the trees before him and the limited space between them, he could imagine Isla moving swiftly between them and climbing them effortlessly. He looked up, wondering if there was anything living in the high branches like the large cats of Rennet. Things he hadn't even known about until he'd had her dreams.

He hadn't had any more. They tended to happen when they were close, and he missed her. She had her tasks to do. He hoped that Calder didn't have her locked away somewhere trying to force the Rohen to talk.

Had Hendra ever just approached the Rohen and asked what they wanted? Or did she not care? "Where is Alice?" he asked.

"Busy," Beth said, stepping down into the trees. He followed.

"Where are we on Draroh?"

"Near the chief," she said, running her hand around a tree and leaning into it. The scent of the forest filled Gray's senses—the trees, the litter—and he remembered Isla leaning into the wooden walls of a cell and smelling the familiar comfort. When he refocused on the world around him, the child was gone. He stepped forward, wondering if she had disappeared, but he couldn't see any sign of her.

"Beth!" he called.

Another child ran past him, brushing against him as they raced out between the trees. And then he too was lost from sight. Gray wasn't sure why he was out here, but he felt the same comfort as in the library, as though he had to be here. As though his purpose was to learn. But he wasn't sure why.

"You will be telling the story. You are the storyteller." A smaller child had stopped beside him, taking his hand.

"Storyteller?" he asked the child as she squeezed his hand. He wondered when they had appeared and what they were doing. Were they Readers?

"In a way," she said and, with a smile, disappeared to join the others ahead of her.

"Storyteller?" he mused again, standing at the edge of the forest. He stepped up to the nearest tree and ran his hand over the bark, wondering if the children felt anything different from what he could feel.

"The Sparrow's song is true," a voice said softly behind him, and he turned to the minister. "You have heard those words before, have you not?"

Gray bowed his head.

"We all have a purpose in this world," the minister said, turning back towards the house. "There are those who would meet you."

Gray reluctantly left the forest and climbed the steps back to the house. He wondered just how many people needed to see him. Tevia had said there were those waiting. He had thought she meant the minister and his family, but it appeared there were more, and he knew it wouldn't do him any good to try and guess at what they might want from him. He would find out soon enough.

He followed the man back into the house, then through the house to another long corridor and a walkway Gray hadn't seen. He hadn't had the chance to explore the house or its surroundings very much. Not that he really wanted to. He longed to be with the books now that he was back in the house.

At the end of the walkway was a large window looking out over a city. Tall buildings sparkled in the light, green trees and parks dotted amongst them, and he thought it far nicer than the endless buildings and concrete of Rennet. They had found a way to work with the world around them, or at least bring it into their cities.

"Are we that close?" he asked. He hadn't heard any sounds of the city from within the house, and the window shimmered and rippled. "It isn't just there."

"It is closer than you think," the minister replied. He stepped up to the glass and then through it, disappearing from sight. Gray took a deep breath and followed, surrounded by cold, and then he was standing in a large open room. The smooth white walls rippled as he carefully made his way down the wide steps to join the minister in the middle of the room.

"How did you find that?" he asked.

"I..." Gray stammered, trying to take in what might have happened and where he might be.

"Some find it a bit unsettling the first time. There are many gates around the Complex, but we use them more frequently here on Draroh."

Gray nodded, unsure what to say or ask.

"It is the Rohendra that allow such a thing," the minister said, walking ahead and out of the room. Gray followed, unsure at first if his legs would work, but they appeared to.

"You move through the Rohen," he said. "I've done that before. But not quite like this."

"It doesn't allow passage to those it does not want."

"Where are we?" Gray asked as they headed into a wide, white corridor. The floor was polished and, although it could have been any hallway, the tall ceilings and the room they had just left gave the impression of somewhere grand. He wondered then what might have happened if the Sparrow had reached Draroh all that time ago.

"Central," the minister said, continuing on. Gray picked up his pace to keep up with the older man, who was far spritelier than he appeared.

"Hendra..." he started, and the man gave him a dark look. "We are still on Draroh," he said. "The chief?"

"Chief Brown would like to speak with you" the minister said, still marching on.

"I'm not sure what use I will be to him."

"You have met with the Hendra herself," the minister said, not looking around. "You cannot be afraid of an old man."

"I'm not afraid," Gray murmured, "but I do think people are expecting a lot more of me than I can give."

"Just sing your song, Sparrow."

Dekka Brown was not the man Gray had thought he would be. He was older, and clearly very much in charge, although that part Gray had expected. He stood before the desk in an office that reminded Gray of Ebberah's space, although it had more warm wood tones than the stark white of her office.

Several men stood around Chief Brown as they entered. The men bowed their heads to the minister, as the chief raised his eyes to take them in. His gaze lingered on Gray, who bowed his head.

"Your Grace," he murmured.

"Thank you," the chief said to those around him, and they bowed and left the room.

They waited a moment. Gray wondered if they were going to be seated, but the chief of the planet continued to look him over. "This is him," he finally said, and the minister nodded.

Gray wasn't quite sure what he could say or what was expected of him, and so he waited.

"She trusts you," the chief said as though it were a surprise. "The girl," he added as though that answered the question.

"Isla?"

The chief bowed his head.

"I think so—I hope so."

"You don't want to deceive her?"

"No, I don't." Gray hoped he didn't sound as disrespectful as he thought he did.

"So, are you to be the one we need you to be?" the chief asked.

"I'm not sure what you need. Or is it what the Rohendra need?" Gray asked, wondering if he was overstepping some line here. Everyone else seemed to understand what was going on with the Rohen.

"That would be up to Minister Burre. He knows more of what they want than I could even guess at."

"You don't talk with them?" Gray asked, surprised that nearly everyone else here could.

"That is what a minister is for," the chief said, looking as though he couldn't quite understand where Gray was coming from. "You have been staying with him?" Gray nodded. "You've seen the children?"

Gray turned to the man beside him, who gave him a friendly smile and a slight nod of his head. They were not all his children, then. Gray had wondered why he hadn't seen their mother, and yet that wasn't something you asked if you weren't sure. He had just assumed and, now that he was standing here, he felt silly for thinking such a thing. The older man rested a hand on his shoulder.

"Alice is your daughter," Gray said, answering the question he most wanted to ask. "And you share the same skills."

"Have you seen her?" the chief asked.

"No," Gray lied, "not since I've arrived here. I wonder that the Hendra would let her out of her sight."

"She is missing," the chief said. "The rumours are confused, or at least contradictory. But Hendra herself has asked me if I took something of hers when I left Rennet. Has she contacted you?" he asked the minister.

"No," the minister said. "I wonder if something has happened, that no one has contacted me."

"You are not worried."

"I did not know until now, Your Grace, that there might be something to worry about. I hear from Alice from time to time, but her duties with the Hendra keep her busy."

"Hmm," the chief said, turning away from him. Gray wondered just how much he knew. The room was likely monitored. Despite the chief's back to them, he didn't dare turn to the minister.

"Minister," Gray said, looking at him more closely. "Your position is one with the Rohen."

The minister bowed his head. "Not just the children, although that is key."

"If that is the case, why do you need me?"

"It is not a recognised position throughout the Complex. Not everyone understands the Rohen and what they mean to us. What they mean to the continued existence of the Complex."

"And yet you want to send me out like some prophet," Gray murmured.

"That isn't quite what we have planned," the chief said. "There are others working to do what they can for the Rohen, to protect them. Removing the Hendra is what is required."

He sounded like Ebberah. Gray looked at the older man beside him. That wasn't what the Rohen wanted. They wanted the child in charge, and if the Hendra was deposed then that couldn't happen.

"Unless she came to power a different way," the minister whispered.

"How?"

The man gave him a smile, but it didn't make any sense to Gray. The people had been following the Hendra for so long. If they could maintain that until the child they needed was in power, then it would be worth waiting for. They had done this—Alice had done this for them—to allow just such a thing to happen.

"Your Grace," Gray said as the man sat down and then indicated they do the same. Gray looked around him. The minister raised a hand, and two chairs appeared behind them. Gray wanted to ask how it was done; he thought Isla could do the same, but he wasn't clear on what she was either. Something very like Alice—or it might have been that Alice was like Isla.

"I have been led to believe that you will work with us," the chief said.

"I'm not sure what you are working towards or if we are working towards the same thing. Until I know what you want, I'm not sure I can claim to be on a side."

"I understood that Hendra was trying to have you killed."

"At least her Elite appeared to be, but that was related to something from long ago. Not anything of interest here."

"Isn't it? The Sparrow is an important part of our history."

"We didn't make it to Draroh," Gray said, then wondered just what this man knew of his history and who he was.

The chief smiled and interlocked his fingers as he leaned forward onto his elbows on the desk. Gray realised there were far more who knew who he was, what he was doing and what he might be able to do than he would like to admit. He had spent so many years in hiding, so many years tucked away. Or at least it had felt that way. Not nearly as many years as Isla had tried to hide in plain sight. And yet it had been that moment of recognition across a racing pit that had drawn him out of hiding and into this mess. And messy it was—and only getting worse.

He was suddenly more lost than he had been before. He trusted in the Rohen, in the Rohendra, despite what had happened to Isla. They had given to him when he'd asked, and now he was here for a reason. Although he had no idea what Isla was doing or where she was. He could only trust she would find him again, or him her.

Six

Hendra paced her office again. Or was it that she was still pacing after the events of the previous day? The lack of understanding as to what was going on was far more frustrating than she'd thought it could be. She hadn't slept, nor had she had the chance to eat, although she was sure someone had arrived with food. She didn't trust it. She couldn't trust the staff that surrounded her. The people who had always surrounded her. They knew the risks if they betrayed her, and no one had. No one had tried to do anything they shouldn't against a Hendra.

Then she had married Alice, and the world had changed. Despite the hours she had spent trying to work it out, she still didn't have a definitive reason why she had fallen so hard for the woman. What was it about Alice that had singled her out above all others? What had she offered that Hendra had been willing to go against what her father might have planned for her? When she could have married for the strength of the Complex?

Not that she had rushed into any marriage, nor had her father pushed the point. He'd known it would happen at some stage. It had to occur for the continuation of the line. But Hendra hadn't found anyone she'd thought was worth the effort until Alice. And then the woman had poisoned her and her child before disappearing, only to be found dead—but not dead.

Hendra sighed and sat down against the desk just as the door opened and one of the secretaries appeared. The solar system was big, and Alice could be hiding anywhere. She could have countless allies that Hendra couldn't even comprehend. She had so far been unable to even find out how Alice had gotten off Rennet.

"Tell me there is some news," Hendra said without looking up.

"Calder is at the factory," an unexpected voice announced, and she looked up at the general. "You have given him too much."

"He was worth the effort. He has done everything I have asked and more."

"Except he didn't, when you wanted him to return."

She wanted to agree with him, but Calder was her one true ally. "He did."

"Eventually—and with the hummer. He has taken her to the factory. She'll do something."

"Not at the factory, she won't. There is nothing there, and what remains will stop her."

"You saw the footage from the facility, in the tube?"

Hendra nodded.

"It doesn't work," he mumbled.

"Of course it does. All that screaming the hummers report throughout the facilities. She's a hummer, not Rohen. It doesn't work on her as it does the Rohen. We've never had issues elsewhere. Maybe it is just her..." She looked up at him then, thinking about what she was saying, what she had seen. Island Tarle was different from the other hummers. She knew something, or Calder had told her more than Hendra had expected, or he was working with her after all.

She closed her eyes and tried to remember him after the attack. After the horror. It had been difficult to pull him out of there. He might not have remembered being there. Unlike what they had tried with Island, she had openly lied to him when he'd come out of the surgery. They had discussed it often enough, planning his disappearance, removing him from that team and transplanting him into another that she was sure would do what she needed them to. She'd told him the surgery was planned during their assault in the cavern, so that he could disappear. They could claim him dead. They just didn't realise that everyone else would die.

He had asked for her then—Island. He had wondered if she'd survived, and Hendra had told him no. He hadn't seemed that concerned when he'd learnt the truth and assured her that he hadn't become attached. Just like he'd promised he wouldn't when he went in. But that was the sort of thing you couldn't promise. She had seen that with Alice. Just another woman, and yet within a very short space of time, she wasn't. She was so much more. Although Hendra wouldn't have given up the Complex for her, she would have sacrificed anything else.

She took a deep breath and opened her eyes to the general and his concern. Then she stood slowly, walked to the table and sat down.

"You need to look after yourself," he said.

She nodded once, but she knew he was right. She had to ensure this child survived because she might not get the chance at another. But then, Alice had nothing to do with this one in the first place. She stared at the man sitting down opposite her. She hadn't thought of him as someone she could use for such a thing. "The factory," she murmured.

He bowed his head. "They were seen together."

"At the factory?"

"It has been empty for some time."

She nodded slowly. She had ordered it moved when he had disappeared, but that was all she had done. "Where is it?"

"She won't find it."

"I thought if I appeared to be helping then she would be more willing to do as I asked. But she said it isn't possible to make the Rohen do as she wants."

"Is that exactly what she said?"

"No," Hendra murmured. "She said it was not possible."

"But not impossible."

"I don't think now is the time to discuss semantics," Hendra grumbled. "The girl will not do as I want. Whether that is because she can't or because she won't, I don't know."

He bowed his head and stood, clearly waiting for instructions.

"He won't be able to find it," she answered.

The general waited.

"Leave him be," Hendra warned. If Calder was a risk to her, she would be the first to ensure he was dealt with. But at this stage, he was to be left alone.

She watched the general leave, unsure whether he would follow her instructions or chase down the disobedient soldier for himself. She chewed on her lip, walked around her desk and pressed her hand to the comm panel. "Come on, Calder," she whispered, but there was no response. The doubt the general seemed to harbour made more sense, and she wondered if he was right that Calder couldn't be trusted.

She turned and marched out through the lounge, moving quickly through the building and not seeing anyone as usual. Today, that seemed to make her somewhat nervous. She picked up her pace, and then she was standing in the doctor's office. A couple of them were sitting at the desk, deep in discussion. As one of them noticed her, he leapt up and bowed low. The other followed.

"I need you to check this child."

He bowed again while she remained where she was, her heart suddenly pounding. They glanced at each other.

"What do you want checked?" the first, Stone, asked somewhat hesitantly.

She didn't know. Was it to see if the child was human? To see if the child was in fact hers? If everything she had thought about her life and the world had been a lie, then this child might be as well.

"Most new mothers worry," the other said, trying to sound calming, but his words only made her bristle.

"I am not most new mothers. I have been poisoned, which has not happened before, and now show no sign of the metal at all." She took a breath, trying to calm the panic that was building in her chest. "I need to know if this child is..."

"Our last scans showed the baby was healthy," Stone said when she couldn't find the words to finish her sentence.

"Is it a child?" she blurted.

They glanced at each other again. Stone opened his mouth and then closed it.

"I know it is a child," she said. "But it may be something else. Something different. Something alien."

"Sit down," Stone said kindly, taking her by the arm and guiding her into the chair he had been sitting in previously.

"I am not a crazy..."

"I am not even suggesting it," he said, his tone carrying the same re-assurance. She wondered for a moment if she saw something else in his eyes, something different, a fleck of silver. She bit down on her lip and was tempted to flee from the room. If only she had Calder here, standing over her to ensure they would not harm her. Not that anyone would have before. She was safe here. She was Hendra. Except Alice had changed that.

Stone nodded to the other man, who left the room. "I appreciate that you know far more of the universe than I could imagine," he said to her. "I am a man of science, and I am a man open to ideas. You are safe here. Your child is safe." He glanced towards the door as he spoke. "I know that you did not conceive this child with your wife."

She nodded slowly. Anyone with a brain could have worked it out, only she protected secrets like that. Everyone had been led to believe they had melded their DNA and implanted the child. "I was told I could not carry a child."

"And yet you carry a healthy child now."

"But do I?"

He leaned back, the same calm, reassuring smile on his handsome face. Had he always been that attractive, or was she seeing the world differently? "Yes."

She breathed as though for the first time. "Should you test for more anomalies?"

"We don't need to. Unless you want to tell me who the father is and whether there is a chance he carries alien anomalies?"

She shook her head. No one knew who the father of her child was, not even the man himself. And if he thought he did, she would never confirm that. This was her child, her future and the future of the Complex. Calder might be a risk at the moment, but he wasn't hummer or Rohen.

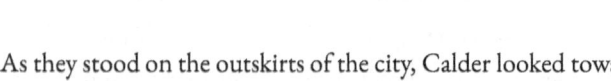

As they stood on the outskirts of the city, Calder looked towards the array of old buildings before him. The car was long gone, Isla was sure reporting to whomever was watching them, where they went and what they were up to. Calder had seemed surprised the dust had disappeared. He was right in that it had been there, and she was sure it hadn't been used. Given the size of the warehouse and the size of the meteor, there was a lot of dust somewhere. She felt the loss of the Rohen and tried not to look like it affected her as much as it did.

Isla breathed out slowly and allowed the world to fill her senses. Allowed the Rohen to tell her what they wanted her to know. She felt the need, but it was emptiness. "They moved it."

"Without telling me? Without telling Hendra? Who would take that risk?"

"Michaels?" she suggested with a shrug.

"It doesn't matter. You want to see it—you can find it."

She looked back at him then from the buildings stretching out before her. The lack of the forest and greenery seemed more apparent. There was so much that this city, this planet and this woman were trying to push from the Complex, and Isla was sick of it.

"You can sense it, can't you?"

She shook her head, but she could feel the absence of Rohen, almost as though it were pressing down on her. Then his hand was around her arm. Her first response was to jerk away from him, but he wasn't holding her hard. It was more for support. As she put her hand up, he let go and she stepped back. "Yes," she said.

He held his hand out to indicate the world before them. "Let's find a meteor."

For a moment, it felt as though it was all in fun, reminding her of the jobs they had done together in the Elite. But when she looked up at him, he wasn't the man she remembered, and she wondered where Gray might be.

She pushed the thought from her mind, looked out across the buildings, turned slowly and put her arms out. Then she stopped, pointed in one direction and started walking, only stopping when he grabbed her arm again.

"Eyes open," he said, his voice uncomfortably familiar again. She did as he said.

"You have to stop that," she muttered, moving ahead and towards the feeling. She wasn't sure how close it was, and it could be that they would need to walk for a day before they found what she was looking for. She wasn't sure what they would do when they found it.

"Stop?" he asked. She did and looked at him.

"What?"

"Stop what?"

"Pretending this is something it isn't—pretending you are someone you aren't. I'm still not sure why you are helping, or even if you are. Or why the Rohen would suggest that you would. I'm not going to pretend with you, Calder. Rick."

"I became something else."

"You were that something before. I know what we had wasn't real. I know what I need to do, and you can't get in the way of that. It doesn't matter what games you and Hendra think you are playing—the Rohen are playing a better game than both of you."

"I'm not playing," he murmured, walking on ahead and then waiting for her. She shivered and then followed.

With every step, the feeling of loss grew. She longed for trees and animals and the hum of the world beneath her fingers, but it wasn't there. Not in any way. She wondered then if this was why the trees weren't growing, why the world looked dead. The buildings that surrounded them looked tired, uncared for, as though they hadn't been lived in or used for some time.

"Where are we?" she asked. "What is this place?"

He looked around and then shrugged. "Some industrial area, perhaps. As the systems improve and technology advances, services, trade and manufacture move closer to the city."

Isla looked behind her at the tall, sparkling buildings reaching up the sky. It was some distance away, but she could still see it. The large block towering over it all was Hendra Central. Things might have moved closer, but she didn't imagine that Hendra would want the sounds of industry that close to her home. Someone was using this space, though; she could sense the people, hear the thud of equipment. If, as she suspected, the Rohen were involved in the revolutionary activities, she didn't think they would be anywhere near here. They would feel the loss—but then if they did, maybe they could find it.

It might do more than just dull their senses and prevent their crossing it. It might prevent them understanding what was on the other side. Isla continued forward, wondering if any of the people she sensed would try to stop them or would be a threat. The duster formed too easily in her hand. Despite the feeling closing in around her, the Rohen was still here.

"Are you really trying to help me?" he asked.

"I think you are helping me," she said.

"Either way, I have some trust issues when it comes to you." He looked pointedly at the duster.

Isla laughed, the sound coming easily and freely. She couldn't stop it. Who was this man trying to be?

"Fair," he muttered.

Once the giggling stopped, Isla focused on the world around her, particularly in front of her. They worked their way between old buildings, through empty hangars, and at one point she put her hand to his arm and he stopped. A ball rolled past the makeshift path they were following between the buildings, and a child chased after it, not seeing them.

Calder looked at her with surprise, and she nodded once. They continued on. She might have known there were people hidden in these buildings, but they didn't know someone else was around. If Hendra had hidden a meteor in the area, they might not be safe, but then maybe they didn't want to draw attention. She did wonder how they had moved so much without being seen.

A man walked towards her. She motioned Calder out of the way, dissolved the duster she was carrying and raised her hand. "Hey," she called. "I think I am very lost."

"Likely, if you are down here," he said, his voice friendly. Then his eyes crinkled with recognition.

Isla waited, hoping this was not going to be the risk she feared it was. She could sense nothing on him, as though the Rohen wasn't there. Her heart rate increased, and she felt as though she had lost a good friend.

"Is there any work around here?" she asked, trying to keep her voice level.

"There was—some business had us moving bags of stuff from one warehouse to another. No roads. Although they could have flown it out, we are likely cheaper."

Isla nodded. "Bags? I heard something about cement or sand or something."

"Don't know what was in it. Just as much filtered through it and out, I think. We were covered in the stuff and can't seem to shift it."

"Oh," she said. "I hope it wasn't something dangerous. I had this job offer way back..." She pointed behind her.

"What do you mean dangerous?" he interrupted, his eyes wide. "You think we're expendable?"

"I don't," she said.

"I'd stay away from that building down there," he said, pointing to the next one along. Isla could feel the emptiness, but it seemed to surround her now, as though she had breathed in his dust and it was blocking any sense of the Rohen.

She held her breath, bowed her head in thanks and turned back towards Calder. When she reached him, a few paces back and hiding in a dark alcove, she wore a mask. She had struggled to create it, struggled to pull the Rohen from the air.

She pointed, and he nodded silently, following her. She inched forward slowly in case there was anyone else about, fearing she wouldn't sense them now that the dust was so thick in the air. Had they really bagged the dust and then employed local help to move it? It could have taken days. It would have taken coordination. Again, she wondered who didn't want Calder to know that it had been moved.

Calder went first into the old building. There was no security, no hint that there was something of worth stored inside, and she wondered if that was part of the plan. If it was stolen, or used by someone else in the building, it would go some way to slow the Rohen and their hold over the Complex. At least in Hendra's eyes, Isla thought. Without the Rohen, the Complex would die.

The door was stiff, and Calder looked around. "There might be a silent alarm," he whispered. There was no sign of lights or wiring or anything of the like that might indicate the door had been opened. But Isla wondered if that was because the Rohen wouldn't work in the area.

Once inside herself, she couldn't understand why she hadn't felt this sooner. Why it wasn't like a beacon from the city. She breathed more easily in the mask. Calder studied it. She wasn't taking it off, and if it stopped her becoming blocked from the Rohen, it didn't matter. But as she saw the realisation in Calder's eyes, her heartbeat sped up. He shook his head slowly, but she knew he would use the information. If not on her, then on another hummer at some other point. She couldn't trust that he wouldn't betray them.

Beyond them, the warehouse was a similar size as the one Calder had taken her to, but it was filled with stacks of sacks, each stuffed with dust. She wanted to get closer but something held her back. There was so much of it. They could use this for more than glass containers and walls of facilities—this could be used to block the Rohen from much of the planet. Or others, she thought as she considered the facility on Oric. Although how they transported it, she had no idea. Could it be that they had other warehouses on other planets—or even here?

"How much?" she asked.

Calder looked across at her.

"How much of this is there?"

"Here?" he asked, looking back at the pile. "A good chunk of meteor."

"And the other chunk?" she asked.

"Already used."

"Not sitting in other warehouses then?"

He shook his head. But then he looked around. They had moved this without telling him; there was a very good chance that there were other such buildings he didn't know about either.

"Just how much do you think you are in control of this situation?" she asked.

"I am more in control than you are."

"No, you're not," she said, wishing she could form another duster. But the Rohen was absent from the space. It wasn't even that they weren't there but that they struggled to reach her in this space. They were absent. There was nothing. "You think you have been Hendra's right-hand man, but she is either keeping things from you or someone else is working around her, and you weren't able to stop that."

"She is my first priority," he grumbled, walking towards the piles of sacks. They were just on the floor, no pallets, no mechanism to remove them from the warehouse or carry them elsewhere.

Isla wondered how far one bag went. Was there only a little in the glass? Only a bag to build a facility that would stop the Rohen? They could really contain the Rohen with this, or at least keep mankind from the Rohen. Isla shivered.

"Who?" he asked, drawing her attention.

"Excuse me?" she asked, stepping back. How could she prevent this? How could she destroy a meteor?

"Who would be working around the Hendra? Who would she allow the power to do that?"

Isla studied him then as he looked over the piles of bags.

"Did you think you were the only one?"

He turned his dark, angry features on her. "I am her creation," he said, although he didn't sound pleased by the idea.

"How did she do that?" Isla asked, stepping forward, curious how this man had become who he was.

He shrugged then and looked back to the bags.

"You led us in," she muttered. She saw his back straighten, his body tense. "You were there. Maybe I wasn't the only body dragged from the field that day."

"I wasn't there."

Isla sighed, but she didn't push it. He had his version of events and, like her, he would believe what he had been told until he didn't. Whether Hendra had dragged him from the field or she had him doing something else at the time, she would never know, and it might be that he wouldn't either.

"So how do we end this?" she asked, pointing to the warehouse.

"I'm not sure I want that."

"I do, and I know of others who have tasked us with this."

"You. They asked you."

"And they said you would help."

"Why would you think I would help you? Part of me would still rather see you dead."

Isla looked up then, wondering if that was true. But she could see his hesitation. Kalli might be long gone from this man, but there was a curiosity as to what came next, as to why the enemy he had been fighting for years without even realising they existed would think that he would help them.

"How did they break it down?"

"I don't know. Maybe mining equipment. They used explosives in space to break it into chunks."

"And you think it all came here?"

"Yes," he said, certainty in his voice. "It was a direction from the Hendra. There are very few of us who know the truth."

"Your version of the truth," Isla said, and he glared at her. "I need to get out. I can't cope with the lack of..." She headed for the door, unable to finish. What had been difficult had become overwhelming, and she could only think of the facility in Oric. "What happened in Oric? Did you find out?"

He shook his head. She wondered if she should be worried, or if he was worried about the lack of understanding as to what had gone on there. That the Rohen and the people had disappeared. Maybe there were other ways for the Rohen to help.

"You have tested it, haven't you—to see what it is made of? Michaels would understand it. Where is he? Still at the garden site?"

"I don't know where he might have gone, and I assume he or someone on his team tested something. They just thought it was sand. We didn't tell them where it was from."

"But he would have worked it out," she insisted. "He knew of the garden. He has been studying the Rohen for years. He would understand that something in that sand prevented movement. Contained them, just as Hendra wanted. What is it? What element?"

"We don't know. It is foreign to our system."

"And alien to the Rohen." She had thought of bringing Michaels with her when they'd first left the garden, but he had stayed to see what he could find. If they knew more of this, if she could discover what it was that made it work, she might be able to find a way to destroy it. She looked around the warehouse again. There was nothing to indicate what this might be, what it might be used for or who might have stored it here. There were no signs to warn of danger or flammability. She wondered then if anyone worried.

The man she had met in the street hadn't seemed to until she'd questioned the possibility, and then he'd only worried when she'd raised the possible dangers. Was he concerned? These people were desperate living out here, working on whatever they could get. He would only have considered the money he would have earned from the job, not the risks. And how dangerous could it be moving bags of sand?

Isla looked at the fine dusting of grey-green powder over the floor. The only sand she really knew was on Urgway, and it was crimson. Maybe there were other forms on other planets, but it was large, granular stuff. This was fine, like it had been manufactured somewhere, something created for use rather than collected. She wondered why no one was questioning it more. But then, they were doing all sorts of things in those facilities and laboratories, with people as well as Rohen. They would question very little.

The silver Rohen man-like forms had been able to move through the glass and out again while not understanding why the other couldn't move through it.

"Ahh!" she cried through the mask.

"What is it?" Calder asked.

"There are too many unknowns, too many questions. I can't answer them."

"Do you need to? You were only tasked with finding it."

"But why is it important? Why does it work, how do we stop it working, or from being used? Why does it work on some Rohen but not all?"

"What do you mean by not all Rohen?" he asked, and she bit her lip.

"Can we please get out of here?"

He nodded towards the door, and she headed quickly towards it. She needed to be far from here, far from the cling of the fine powder.

Seven

The sound of engines above them drowned out any sense of loss Isla was feeling as they worked their way between the old buildings. She still wore the mask, fearful any dust she might inhale would sever her link with the Rohen. Calder's hand was on her back, pushing her along, and then they were standing in the middle of empty space. She wasn't sure if one of the buildings had collapsed at some point or if it had been an open area in the first place; either way, the ship that hovered over them reminded her of her dragonfly. She wondered where it might be and whether she could ever retrieve what she had left on it.

She was tempted to run, but Calder had her by the arm. He gave a shake of his head. This was his team, his idea—or it was better to go with it. She was dragged out of the way by Calder as the ship hovered over the ground. A gangway dropped down from the belly of the ship, and she was directed up it before she had the chance to think about another option.

Calder directed her into a seat. She belted in as they lifted into the air, and he disappeared into the cockpit. The soldier opposite looked her over as though unsure what to do with her. She nodded once and lifted the mask from her face. As she sat it down next to her, allowing it to disappear into the seat, she felt the relief of the Rohen around her. She might have some dust particles clinging to her clothing, but it wasn't enough to prevent her from feeling it now. Maybe they could work around small particles.

"Where are we going?" she asked the soldier, but he continued to stare at her without answering the question.

She could simply disappear from the ship. She wondered what he would report if she did so. Isla had managed to move before, and she could go anywhere she wanted. But right now she needed Calder to learn all she could of the meteor, get access to the science and find out what it was and what they could do with it.

Calder returned not long after and sat beside her, not bothering to belt himself in. She was going to ask where they were going when they slowed and came in to land. Likely they were in Hendra Central. They had not been very forthcoming with Hendra, and Isla had been surprised even Calder hadn't been as open with the leader as she had expected him to be.

The gangway lowered. Isla unbelted and walked down ahead of Calder, his hand again on her back directing her. The hangar still looked and smelt the same. The noise of engines, the banging of tools on metal, mechanics calling across the space and working on various ships—it all sounded familiar and comfortable. The occasional shout as something was dropped or something sparked took her back to a different life.

"Welcome back, Sergeant," someone called as they walked towards the lifts. Isla almost saluted in return. But she wasn't Elite anymore. She wasn't one of these men. In fact, she was trying desperately to find a way to stop them. Even if the Hendra thought there was some chance Isla was working for her, she was really working for the Complex. Trying to find a way to save it from the woman who thought she was in control.

Isla nodded her head instead, and the man grinned and turned back to his work.

"I thought you were some famous criminal," the soldier she had sat across from muttered behind her.

"She was better known in these parts as Elite," Calder said. She was surprised he would voice such a thing even if he believed it, which she wasn't sure he did. He appeared less stern when he entered the lift, turned and looked her over.

"You are not him," she mumbled, more to remind herself she couldn't trust him. His face fell a little. Was he starting to believe his own lies?

When they exited the lift, she was surprised to find they were on the Elite residential level, nowhere near Hendra and her offices, nor even Calder's office.

"I thought you might appreciate a shower and change of clothes. Who knows what that dust might have done to you."

She nodded her thanks and looked along the familiar corridor. She had been bunking in near his office, one of those unknown rooms like the one Alice had thought was secret but wasn't. Isla wondered just what the woman did know and what she was doing now with that knowledge.

Soldiers moved along the corridor, looking her over as though wondering who she might be, then caught sight of Calder. They stood to attention and saluted. Calder nodded his head, and Isla entered what had been her shared room for so many years. It was just the same and yet didn't feel familiar in any way. She came back out and looked down the hall towards the communal bathroom.

The room was empty when she caught sight of herself in the mirror. She was covered in dust; it was through her hair and over her clothes. She ran a hand over her hair and then looked at the fine dust on her fingers. She sat her hand down against the cool metal bay of sinks and could still feel the Rohen, the heartbeat of the universe humming away beneath her fingertips. Maybe it wasn't the dust—maybe it wasn't what they had discovered but something else in that area that had blocked her. Calder appeared in the mirror behind her, and she jumped.

"Do you want me to find you some fresh clothes?" he asked.

She shook her head. She didn't want to look like those around her, dressed as Elite, as a soldier. He bowed his head and left.

Isla headed into the first shower bay, removed her clothes and piled them neatly together. She might be able to learn something from the dust she had collected. She raised her hand before the panel and the hot, steaming water started instantly. She sighed at the relief of the water. She hadn't taken much time of late to really enjoy anything. Closing her eyes, she leaned back under the stream and ran her fingers through her hair.

"Where are the scars?" Calder asked, his voice low and far too close.

Isla's eyes flew open to find him standing directly in front of her, still in his boots in the shower bay as though he had looked and then stepped in. She stopped the water instantly and wrapped the hum of the universe around her, covering herself completely in fresh clothing. Although, her wet hair hung limp down her back. He staggered back, stumbling over his feet as he tried to get out of the shower bay. He tripped over the lip, banged against the door and then leaned heavily into the wall.

"How did you know I was scarred?" she asked.

"I saw..." He stopped and blushed a deep red. Was he embarrassed that he had seen her or that he'd been caught?

"You claimed you weren't there," she said.

"I saw the photos and the footage of you relearning what you were, what had happened."

"You saw me learning the lies Hendra wanted me to share."

He looked away. "They tried to remove the scars to some degree, but they wouldn't heal."

Isla nodded, understanding that her need to have the reminder had been part of the reason her scars hadn't healed. Maybe the Rohen needed her to have a reminder, to help her remember when it was time.

"How?" he stammered.

"I have skills with ointments and the like."

"I knew that, but how?"

"It was time," she said. As she stepped forward, he stepped back as though somewhat worried about what she might do. Or had he finally realised that she was more than he had thought?

He waved a hand to indicate her clothing. "How did you do that?"

"Why were you in my shower?" she shot back. She didn't owe him anything. No matter what help he might be, she wasn't sharing all her skills with him.

An explosion rocked the building, and he ran for the door. A towel formed in her hand. She ruffled her hair, running her fingers through it and pulling it back as she followed. People ran in all directions, and it wasn't until she was chasing the distant figure of Calder along the hallway, trying to get around the people filling the space, that she remembered her clothes and the dust she had hoped to gather.

Someone slowed and bowed their head to her. Although she didn't recognise the woman, she saw the glint of silver in her eye as she pushed her way towards the bathroom. Isla stopped and watched her go, and then someone was pushing her back the other way and she was swept away in the thick of the movement flowing towards the lifts. She had lost sight of Calder and wondered if that would help her or if it would be a problem that she was out here on her own.

Hendra. If Central was under attack, then he would go to her first. She closed her eyes and walked into the Hendra's office. Hendra was standing by her desk, the general at her side, as they read something on a panel. She looked up as Calder pushed through the door, and he almost knocked Isla over as he raced forward. Then he stopped, appearing flustered and panicked. It wasn't something he seemed to allow others to see.

He stepped away from Isla as though she were something else. His mouth opened and closed like a fish out of water, unsure what to ask. She wondered if he knew of yet more secret passages through the building. They had been some distance from the Hendra's office.

"What do we know?" Isla asked.

"Nothing," the general grumbled.

"Nothing you want to share, or you don't know anything?" she growled.

"Explosions is all we know."

"In the building?" Calder asked, regaining his senses.

The general looked at him as though wondering if he should tell him anything, and she wondered if Calder had lost the trust of the people he was so sure he was working for.

"Who is doing this?" he asked.

The general handed him the panel. He looked at it, pressed something and watched again before he held it out to Isla. Then he paused. She waited and, when he nodded once, she took it. She watched a nondescript woman—who could even have been the same woman she had passed in the hallway—put a bag down at her feet as she checked a device in her hand. Then the woman walked off, leaving the bag, and before she was even a few steps away, it exploded. Through the dust, Isla could see the windows shattered and people running, some injured from the blast.

"Where is this?" she asked.

"The lobby," Calder answered.

"Deliberate," Isla mused aloud. "I didn't think they were targeting you. Or they are aware of the facility located on-site."

The Hendra glared at her, but said nothing.

"These idiots don't know what they are doing," the general growled. "They want change, but they don't know what that would mean. They are just trying to get attention. The best way to get attention is to target the centre of the Complex."

Another explosion sounded further away, but it rumbled through Isla—and then another and another. She raced towards the window, only Calder pulled her back. She turned to glare at him, and he released her instantly. He appeared unsure of her, not just that she was a hummer and something he could use to further his career, but something more. Something he didn't understand.

She didn't know if that made her more dangerous in his eyes and therefore something more likely to need to be disposed of. But in recent moments, he truly seemed more afraid of her than wanting to kill her, and fear did strange things to men.

"There," he said, moving around her and pointing to the plumes of smoke rising from the city.

Several other explosions followed, but they were further out and she couldn't sense them. Large flashes of flame and then streams of dark smoke rose into the air. They were spaced close together around the city and beyond. Another coordinated attack.

"How the...?" the general asked, focusing further out, and then he turned his back to the window.

Isla focused on where he had been looking. Was that the warehouse they had found? Was it enough to destroy what was there, and had she helped them find it?

"I have things to do," the general murmured.

"I want the building secured," the Hendra called after him.

"It is overflowing with soldiers," he replied and was gone.

Isla looked back out the window, wondering just who was involved with this. Were the Rohen working to make the Complex what it needed to be once more, or were they working against the Hendra? When she looked away from the window, Calder was watching her, and she couldn't read what he might be thinking at all.

Eight

Hendra wanted to hide. She wasn't sure where the feeling had come from, but it was starting to overwhelm her. She put her hand to her belly, wondering again at what Stone had said, and looked up to find Calder watching her. He had run straight to her when the attack had begun, but he had brought the girl with him.

Hendra looked at Isla standing by the window. She noticed Calder glance towards the girl, but there was a hesitation in the way he looked at her. Hendra tried to remember the moment he burst through the door, and she thought the girl had already been standing there. Had she come in first? Had she thought that Hendra was a threat, or under threat?

"I think it is a message," Isla said, focusing in a particular direction. Calder watched her as though she might be the threat. Would he have brought her here if she was? "Your child is safe," she said, and Hendra realised her hands were still on her belly despite the girl not looking in her direction.

"You said that before."

"She is everything."

Hendra wanted desperately to know how this woman—this girl—could know so much. She was still the young woman they had dragged from the battlefield. Hendra glanced at the tall man who had moved in closer to her—was Calder protecting her? He had also been dragged from that same field, not that he knew it, and she was sure he hadn't been seen by Isla. She had asked too often where he was, where he had been. Hendra herself had overseen the work required to make her what she needed to be, and yet she was far more than Hendra had ever thought she could be.

Calder nudged the woman in the back of the shoulder, but she was calm when she turned to take him in. He stepped back. "Tell her what you know," he murmured, and for a moment Hendra thought he was directing her, although it wasn't the usual strong direction she saw in him.

"Not enough," Isla said. "But as I told you before, your child is important."

"Then why is this happening?" Hendra indicated out the window.

"Because you are trying to unbalance the Complex."

"I *am* the Rohendra Complex," she growled.

The girl smiled. "You and I both know that is not right."

"You could help," Hendra snapped, unsure what help she would want from this woman.

"I am helping," Isla said. "Only I'm not here to help you. It will help you in the long term. Maybe."

Calder growled something before Hendra could even open her mouth.

"I need to check the... something," Isla said to Calder, turning away from Hendra. She wanted to wrench the girl's attention back. Before she could consider how to do that, Isla disappeared.

Hendra stared at the space she had occupied as Calder swung for the door. "You should have killed her," she stammered once she regained her senses. Just what connection did Isla have with the Rohen that she could just disappear?

"I know where she is," he said, running from the room.

"You know what you need to do when you find her," Hendra directed.

"It isn't safe," he replied as he pulled her office door shut.

"For whom?" Hendra asked as she stood in the empty office. Her building had just been attacked, her city bombed, and he should have been watching over her and her child rather than running after the girl.

She sighed as she moved closer to the window, hoping to see some sign of normality returning to the world beyond, but it already appeared just as it always had, other than the plumes of smoke rising up across the city. Far more of them than she'd realised. She had to discover who was responsible for this. It wasn't the people; there was no reason for them to do this. None. Hendra did everything for the Complex, and it ran perfectly.

She waited, watching out over the city as she wondered where the general thought he would discover the truth and how long until he returned. The Rohen were far more involved than she had thought them brave enough to be. She had underestimated them before and had sworn she'd learnt from that, but she was starting to wonder if she had become complacent again. It had—*they* had—been a major part of the Complex for so long that they were hard to contain. But she had a way.

Gray wondered just what these people thought he could do for them. He watched the minister work through his papers at the desk while he flipped through the pages of another book. It didn't quite have the same hold over him as before, and he wondered if it had worn off.

He was still amazed that he had the understanding he did and at the images that played out above the page as he glanced over the words. It was a deeper experience than when he had read anything else—than when he had tried to read. As his finger ran over the thick character that marked the beginning of a section on the page before him, he wondered what Isla would make of this.

He was reminded of her understanding that the glitches in the lab were something more even though she couldn't read them. He missed her, and there were times he feared he wouldn't ever get to see her again. He thought they were training him for something, like the children he tended to only see at mealtimes. They were certainly learning their place in the Complex—whether that was to serve the Rohen or the appearance of it, he wasn't sure. The older man muttered something as he dipped the wooden pen into the ink and continued his scratching.

Was this his future? Reading the words of the Rohendra, learning what they were, what they needed? Advising accordingly so that mankind followed and the balance continued? Odd how quickly he understood that the Rohen wanted balance, and that was what was important. No individual was worth more than another, but they weren't individuals.

Gray looked over the bookcases and closed the book in his hand. Standing slowly, he stretched his arms out to the sides and rotated his shoulders.

"Soon," the minister said.

"Pardon?"

"You will learn soon enough."

"What will I learn?" he asked.

"What you need to know. What you want to know."

"Do you know what I want to know, or what you think I need to know?" Gray asked, studying the old man's bent back.

"She'll tell you. You already know the answers. Many are contained within these pages." He swept a hand towards the bookcases without lifting his attention from the work before him. "You have the understanding, and when required you will become what you need to be."

"A minister of Rohendra?"

The old man laughed as he looked up and shook his head. "Go and stretch your legs. Breathe in the scent of the forest."

Gray nodded and headed out into the surrounding trees. The size of them still surprised him and took him to a place he didn't quite understand, like the dreams of Isla's world. He found himself searching for the cats again.

He stepped down amongst the broad trees and wondered if there was any risk they could fall and crush the house. But he didn't think the Rohen would allow that to happen. He leaned against a trunk, ran his fingers over the rough bark, put his nose to it and breathed in. Again, Isla came to mind. As the scent overwhelmed him, he laughed at the idea of tasting it. Instead, he stepped back and looked up into the branches far too high to reach, then turned and walked further into the forest.

After only a few steps, he had no idea where the house was or which way led back to it. It all looked the same, but he wasn't worried about getting lost. He continued along what looked like a worn path where the children had run previously. He ran his fingers over the trunks as he walked, almost sensing that they had done the same as they had gone before him.

Gray focused on the world around him as he walked, not thinking of anything but the trees and the plants and the smell of the wood. It was almost alive to his senses. Then he thought he saw a silver thread and followed it around a tree to find a low silver plant. Rohen. He gently rubbed a leaf between his fingers and heard shouting in the distance. The angry shouts of children, not someone playing a game and not how he had heard them talking to each other previously.

He moved quickly towards the noise to find one boy screaming at Beth. Several of the others were trying to hold him back, but he was determined to reach her. The boy's face was red with rage and, although he had spent time with all of them, Gray couldn't remember the boy's name. Without hesitation, he put himself between them. The other boys maintained their hold on him. He appeared desperate to get around Gray to the girl, who now clung to the back of his shirt.

"What is going on here?" Gray asked.

"She is strange!" the boy screamed.

"I thought all of you were special in some way."

The girl behind him whispered something, but he couldn't make it out.

"They are all crazy," the boy continued, "but she is weird."

"I like weird," Gray said.

"You'd have to here," the boy growled, still tugging at the hold of the other boys.

"Why are you here?" Gray asked, trying to keep his voice level and calm. He wasn't good with children. He was fine with Reilly's son, but that was different. He'd been there when the kid was born. "Why are you living with the minister?"

"Nowhere else to go, same as most here. Lost family or disowned."

Gray wondered about the little girl behind him. Had her family given her away? She seemed happy enough. Usually.

"What is the problem right now?" Gray asked, trying to pin down why this boy was still trying to reach Beth despite the conversation and the other boys hanging on his arms. He wanted them to let go, but he had no idea what the boy might do.

"She is not human," the boy spat.

"We live amongst many species," Gray said, wondering why that was an issue. Although looking at all the children standing around the small clearing, they were all human. He had yet to see any of the other species here.

"She's different, not another species. She's metal!"

"Ok," Gray said, stepping forward and reaching for the boy's shoulders. "Let's just calm down."

"Metal, like a machine," the boy stammered, and Gray realised he was afraid.

"You understand the Rohen," he said to the boy. "You read about the metal."

The boy shook his head. "Not like this—not like her."

Gray turned to take in the girl who had been standing behind him, and there was a cry from one of the others. The boy broke free, shouldered Gray hard out of the way and lunged for Beth. Just before he reached her, a wall of Rohen flowed from the ground to block his access to her. Gray was reminded of the walls changing in the mine as they were finding their way out when Calder had tried to kill Isla.

The boy stopped for the first time, his eyes wide with fear as he watched the rippling wall shimmer between them. "I told you," he whispered. But Gray doubted this was Beth's doing. The Rohen itself was protecting the girl. She was important, far more important than Gray and his reading could ever be. He opened his mouth to tell the boy just that when the wall crashed down over him and disappeared into the ground, the boy gone.

Beth sighed, and a murmur went through the children. Gray stepped forward, but there was nothing there—no sign of the Rohen or of the boy.

"I'll tell the minister," one of the older ones who had been holding onto him said, running ahead.

"Where?" Gray stammered, wondering if the Rohen was capable of killing a child just because he threatened one of their own.

"We are to serve," one of the others said. "He will serve a different way."

"He did not understand what he was," Beth said, looking at the place where the boy had been. Her eyes sad, she sighed again. She then lifted those sad eyes to him, and the hope he had felt earlier seemed to disappear. "He will," she added, taking his hand. "I will lead you back."

"I'm not lost," Gray said, but he was, and he was grateful for the children who surrounded him as they walked through the forest together.

Nine

Isla walked through the remains of the warehouse. She could sense the dust, but she could also sense the Rohen. There was a moment of fear as she looked around, wondering what that would mean. Maybe now that it was spread so far around the city, it no longer had the impact it had as piles of sand. She moved through the debris, sensing the other people looking over the damage moving in closer. Many of the buildings she had moved between previously were gone. It was a mess of steel and twisted metal. But she could breathe.

She turned to talk to someone coming up behind her, but they stood back looking over the destruction, almost surprised that she was there—as though maybe she was responsible.

She wondered then if anyone had seen who might have been around. Was it the people led by the disguised Rohen? Again, she wondered at the number of hummers or those working with the Rohen. Someone like her, someone understanding what was needed. She knew this place had been hit amongst the others the moment the smoke started to rise from the city surrounds.

She knew these attacks had started with the aim of destroying the warehouse. She stepped forward, wondering if there was a chance of something left, some clue to prove her theory or something of the dust. But as she worked her way through the debris, she knew it was spread far enough that it wasn't the risk it had been. She only hoped that Calder hadn't been lying and that there wasn't any more; but then, she didn't think he was as fully across the state of play as he thought he was.

The hum of the approaching ship moved through her bones, and the dust swirled around her.

"You shouldn't be here," Calder called from the open hatch, motioning her forward. "It isn't safe."

"It is much safer now than it was," she returned, making no move to join him on the ship.

It hovered lower, and he leapt out. With a wave of his hand, it lifted higher into the sky. Isla was surprised he was still as strong as he had been all those years ago. Calder always seemed so much older than Kalli, and although he wasn't that much older than her, he came across as an old soldier.

He worked his way through the debris towards her, and when she stepped out of reach, he raised a duster.

"You know I'm not responsible for this," she said. Although, in many ways she was. She had found what she had been sent to find, and the Rohen had found a way to remove the threat.

The duster remained pointed at her. "You need to return with me. We don't know who else is out here. It isn't safe for you."

"You never cared about my safety before," she said, stepping over a crumbled wall and reaching for the duster in his hand.

As she touched the end of it, it dissolved, and he staggered back.

"What are you?" he asked.

Her earlier uncertainty and fear disappeared with the weapon. "I am a hummer," she said.

"I don't understand what that is," he stammered.

"I'm just learning," she replied, "to feel the hum." She felt the certainty of it as she said it. She returned the duster, holding it out, and he looked at it for an age before he took it.

"And me?"

"I'm not sure, but the Rohen assures me you will help."

"Hendra?"

"Is important, but not what she thinks she is."

"The child," he said. "My child."

"She was never yours." Isla wanted to reach out and pat his arm, but she didn't. "She always belonged to the Rohendra."

Isla looked back over the desolation around her, the dust floating in the air. Had they really broken it down to such a size, or was this only part of it? There were no signs of the bags, no hint as to what had been in them, and yet she doubted that it had burnt away, no matter the heat. If it had been used in the making of the glass, it might have melted together. She could only see the particles floating in the air. Despite her earlier fear that she might breathe it in, it appeared easier to handle, as though the particles slowly disappeared as they were dealt with by the Rohen. It hadn't been that long since the explosions, and the world was cool around her. Nothing burned. Isla looked around again, wondering if they had been mistaken and there hadn't been an explosion after all.

"Will you come with me?" Calder asked, and she could hear the nervousness in his voice. Was it because of her, or something else? She studied him as the ship he had arrived in swept over the area and back towards them.

She shook her head. She wasn't sure where she was meant to go next. She had done as she had been asked. She wanted to go home, back to the trees, and check on the colony. But she was sure the Rohen had other plans, other tasks. She would wait.

Calder waved towards the ship, which then flew past them and away.

"Don't you need to report the loss to the Hendra?"

"I have the feeling she already knows," he said, looking around. "Or she knew it was somewhere else the entire time."

"Not all here?" Isla asked, but she knew it had been. She looked up into the bright light of the sky. Somewhere far above them, more meteors rotated around their strange axis.

Was there a power in that, something she didn't understand? Would they be willing to try and capture another, bring it down to dust and pebbles and continue the work? Or would it move on—or the Rohen learn where it was, what it was, and send them on their way?

Isla sighed, picking her way back into the centre of the warehouse and looking at the ground. Squatting over the hard cement floor, she ran her fingers through what remained of the dust.

"Is that dangerous?" Calder asked. When she looked up, he indicated his face in a circular motion, pointing to the mask.

"Not anymore. I think it was the amount of it, and whatever was done to the glass. It is time to free the rest," she said, standing up.

"The rest of what? The Rohen?"

"All that metal trapped in cylinders in lost and forgotten places."

"They aren't forgotten, and there are hundreds of them. Do you expect to go around every one? Most of them are empty."

"And who have you left in them?" She thought of the girl in a cage in a facility crumbling away on Oric. "How many of them are made with this dust?"

He shook his head. But then he looked around. Maybe he didn't know as much as he thought he did.

Another rumble moved beneath her feet. Calder stepped in too close. Isla could hear people running from the area, but she wasn't sure where the next attack might be. They could be running into anything, unless they had been involved.

"Hummers?" she asked.

"I don't know what you want, or what I can give you."

Another explosion shook the world. What could she do to help? How could she make any difference and assist in ensuring the balance continued? She thought again of the girl in the cage that the other soldier had mentioned. She closed her eyes, then opened them to the burnt remains of the facility. Much of the entrance had collapsed. Would the Rohen have allowed this to happen?

"What the...?" Calder asked behind her. She jumped and turned to take him in, looking over the remains of the facility before them, the darkness creeping in around them. "How?" he asked as he let go of her shirt.

"You didn't have to come," she said.

"I didn't mean to." He sounded like a lost child. "I thought you were going to run—I just managed to grab your shirt and then we were here."

"Oric," she said, looking over the building before them again. She moved forward slowly, ducking under the fallen doorway and into the dark.

A snap sounded behind her, and the space lit up with an orange glow. Calder's hand appeared over her shoulder, holding out the Elite-issue glow stick. It was going to take some effort to work their way through the space, but she could feel the Rohen in the surrounds; that was enough to reassure her that there wasn't any of the meteor dust here. Hopefully it meant she wasn't going to find the burnt remains of a girl in a cage in some dark corner somewhere.

She took the light and he cracked another, coming to stand beside her. She longed for her old uniform. As she brushed the light against her clothes, a hook formed to hold it, freeing her hands to climb through the small gaps between the fallen ceiling and buckled walls, into the space beyond.

Once they made it through to the main laboratory, she stopped. It was just the same as all the others. So many tall cylinders of glass. They must have made quite a number, as they had with all the glass containers to keep the smaller samples of Rohen in. And where was all the Rohen coming from? She was thankful for the silence. "What did she really think she would learn here?" Isla wondered aloud.

"What it wanted. How we could make it do as she needed it to."

"It was doing what the Complex needed, and therefore what Hendra needed. Why can't she understand that we have to work together? Her and us."

"Us?" he asked.

Isla nodded slowly, but she wasn't sure where the word had come from. She wasn't Rohen, and yet she was. She was part of the Rohendra Complex. In many ways, they were all Rohen.

"Let's keep looking," she said as she moved ahead, running her fingers over the soot that had settled on the panels. There didn't appear to be any real damage here. The smoke had come through, but not the fire. There was nothing contained in the tubes, and she wondered if the scientists had released the Rohen at the first sign of attack and then run, as they had in the laboratory she had visited before. There was no sign of anywhere they might have kept a hummer outside of a glass tube, but they couldn't keep them locked away all the time. Isla pulled at a door towards the back of the building. It was reluctant to give, and the roof started to collapse above her as it opened. Calder pulled her back.

"I don't think we need to go any further."

"Or you don't want me to see what might be beyond this. What else could you do?"

He reluctantly let her go, and she held the light up to look through the slowly settling dust on the other side of the door. Much of the roof had collapsed, and a large chunk of stone lay across the doorway. When she put her hand to it, it was gone. The Rohen was almost visible in the dust. She was sure that she could make out silvery shapes in the odd light as she raised the stick and tried to light the far corners of the room.

She stepped forward as a cage came into view. Calder's hand was tight around her arm, but she shook him off and climbed over what was left of the furniture. The stench of burnt wood filling her senses, she stopped to look around the space. The furniture had been damaged; the roof had fallen in and exposed the night sky in some areas. Had they been exploring that long? There was clear fire damage to the walls as well. Isla raced forward, almost falling over bits of stone that lay across the floor. She reached the cage. The door had been prised off, and she pulled it out of the way.

The cage was only just big enough to stand in. She could have sat or squatted, but her legs would have been pushed up under her chin. Sleeping would have been impossible. She put her hands to the flat bars, the openings not quite big enough to get a limb through but certainly enough to see the world around her. They were cold. She could feel the sadness in the metal, and to some degree the Rohen. Why had they allowed this to happen? Were they waiting to see what the Hendra would do? Use it as evidence against her?

There was nothing there. She hoped the Rohen had freed the girl before the fire started or before the attack even took place. Maybe the scientists took her with them, but that didn't mean she was safe.

"Where is she?" Isla asked.

Calder shook his head, looking around the space. She wondered if he really knew the conditions they were kept in and whether this would have been her fate in the end. That the glass cell wasn't enough for her, that she wasn't able to get what they needed from the Rohen. Isla didn't think any of them would be able to get the answers Hendra wanted—not in all the facilities dotted around the solar system—because they weren't out there. They didn't exist.

"I don't believe that you can help me," she said, looking back at Calder as he kicked over some piles of burnt things in the middle of the space.

Something creaked. He looked up and moved quickly towards her, then barrelled her into the small cell.

He was pressed against her, and she tried not to breathe in the scent of him or focus on the feel of his hard chest against her as the ceiling buckled again.

"They will protect you," he said.

"They may not," she replied. "I might not be any use to anyone anymore."

Ten

Gray stood at the back of the room watching the children read. They all appeared to have the same book, and it was one he had read himself at some point over the last few days—or was it longer than that? He had no real idea of how long he had been here or if he was experiencing a different kind of reality, as he had when they'd been lost in the garden above and beneath the ground in Urgway. He wondered if Michaels was still watching through the window, waiting for it to reappear.

"He's not helping her," Beth murmured. Gray refocused on the child and wondered what she was getting from the book that he hadn't. When he came to stand beside her, she sat with the book closed, both hands across it and eyes closed.

"It is as it is," Alice said from her seat at the front of the room. She wasn't really watching the children, but he didn't think they needed watching. Not since the boy had disappeared in the forest. No one had mentioned it, and the minister hadn't asked after him.

An older girl, one Gray hadn't seen since he had first arrived, wrapped her arm around Beth. He wasn't sure if she had been in the classroom with her or had just arrived. Alice still hadn't looked up.

"She should come here," Beth whispered.

"If it is where she should be," Alice continued, but she looked at the girl and then glanced at Gray.

"He would come. He was to help her."

"Who?" Gray asked.

"Please," Beth whispered, her fingers running back and forth across the cover. Then she sighed and rested her head on her hands.

Gray was tempted to run his hand over her back and make sure she was ok. He had come to care for the little one more than he thought he could. Then she was standing and turning for the door.

"You don't need that," a familiar voice said, somewhat annoyed, and his heart stopped.

"You have to stop taking my weapons," another voice growled, but there was something almost friendly to it. Although he wanted to run through the doorway Beth stood in, he waited.

Alice stood slowly and bowed her head to the class. Gray looked back to the door that led directly into the forest from the classroom, and when he looked back she was gone. Maybe she wasn't ready for them to find her just yet.

Gray forced his legs towards the door, and then Beth had him by the hand and was pulling him out into the sun. "You need to help," she directed.

"I think she is quite capable of helping herself."

She pulled him to a stop, but he had already seen her; she looked tired and messy. Was she covered in soot? And then he was standing between the trees with his arms wrapped around Isla. She squeezed him hard back, resting her head against his chest. She smelt of smoke and iron filings.

"What have you been up to?" he asked, trying to sound casual and refusing to let her go. Had it really been that long since he had seen her?

"Oh, this and that. You?"

"Making new friends, learning new languages."

She looked up then. He reluctantly released his hold as she stepped back, but she kept a tight hold of his shirt as she grinned up at him. "Truly?"

"I am quite the student," he quipped. And as she leaned back into him, he focused on Calder. The man didn't appear to have a weapon, for if he did it would surely be pointed at Gray. Instead, he stood with his arms crossed, but he looked somewhat unsettled.

"E'anah," he murmured.

"Why are you here?" Gray asked.

"He's helping me," Isla said against his chest.

"No, he's not," Beth said, standing by the door, her arms crossed in a similar manner as though she weren't going to let him in the house. The other children had come out, and they murmured amongst themselves.

"Are you the teacher or the student?" Calder asked, the cocky tone Gray expected thick on his tongue.

"He is what he is. Gifted," the child said. Isla let go of Gray and stepped up to meet her, taking her hand and looking at her closely.

"Gifted?" she asked.

"You knew he could talk with the Rohen," Beth said, and then she grinned at Gray. "At least he asks, and they give."

"Hmm," Isla said turning to take him in. He felt his cheeks colour. "I would like to know more."

"He wants to know where you have been and if you are well, first."

Isla looked at the child and then back to Gray, and she nodded.

"Thank you, Beth," the minister said, appearing in the doorway. Gray could only assume that Alice had told him of the new arrivals and sent him on his way. He glanced at Isla and studied the unmoving soldier in the forest. He sighed and waved the man forward. "You are welcome, Colonel. Although it is a surprise that you would come so far." He glanced towards Isla again, who looked at the ground. "Beth will show you to a guest room, and then we will talk."

Calder bowed his head to the minister and followed the child, who would glance back suspiciously at him. The minister took in Isla, looking her over as though reading her, and then he took her hands and closed his eyes.

Isla did the same, but she chewed her lip. "I didn't mean to bring him. I wasn't sure where we were coming." The minister pulled her into his arms and held her close.

"You must have needed to be far from where you were."

She nodded, and Gray thought he could see a tear. Then he was up the steps, not sure what to do. "What happened?" he asked.

"Take her into the trees. Take the time to catch up, and then we'll talk."

She nodded and slipped her hand around Gray's arm. She allowed him to lead her back down the stairs to the forest floor, smiling as he led her along the path. She ran her fingers over the trees where he did, and he rested his hand on hers in the crook of his arm. But when they reached where he would have turned towards the clearing, she tugged him in the other direction.

Her hand slipped into his, and he allowed her to lead him through the trees. Before long they were in a part of the forest he hadn't been before. He felt somewhat nervous that he might not be able to find his way back, but then she had found him. After all this time and all this distance. He wasn't even sure he knew where he was, himself.

"Draroh," she whispered, leaning into a tree. She released his hand as she pushed her nose against the bark. She grinned at him, then touched her tongue to it.

"You did not just do that!" He laughed easily for the first time in too long.

"Just to see your reaction. It is so good to smell the forest, feel the heartbeat through the trees."

"Where were you?" he asked. "What happened?"

She turned and smiled up at him as she rested her back against the tree, both palms pushed against the bark.

"I was going to give you some time, but you look like you've had a rough go of it."

She nodded. "Any attacks here?"

He shook his head.

"I guessed as much before I asked. I'm not sure what they are doing."

"The Rohen are behind this, aren't they?"

She nodded. "You guessed that too."

He smiled at her.

"I was so worried you were buried in that building," she said, pushing forward and throwing her arms around him again. "I hoped they would help, but I couldn't feel them—couldn't sense them anywhere near it."

"They turned up, once the lights went out and the ceiling collapsed."

She pulled back then, looking him over, almost patting him down, and he stepped out of her reach.

"I'm ok," he said.

"You are very good at getting shot," she murmured, looking him over rather than in the eye. He took her shoulders.

"I'm fine. Your fungus friends turned up, then Tevia."

"She could enter the facility?" Isla asked, looking at him for the first time. He shook his head. "She said it would hurt."

Isla put a hand to her chest.

"Were you hurt?" he asked.

She leaned forward, rose up and pressed her lips to his. He took a moment, surprised by the move, and pulled back. She blushed and stepped away, shaking her head. "I was looking for others like me," she said, walking between the trees. He waited before he followed.

"Calder?"

"He helped me find the containment. I think the Rohen have taken care of it. In their way," she murmured, not looking back.

"Is this the way?"

She stopped and looked back, appearing confused.

"To the house," he added.

She nodded and turned back to the path. There was so much he was bursting to tell her, and yet he couldn't quite find the words. He tried to watch the back of her head rather than her body as it moved gracefully along the path.

"Why did you bring him with you?"

"I was just trying to get away from where I was."

"Where was that?" Why did his voice sound so sharp?

She shook her head as the house came into view. Why was he wasting what small amount of time they had together?

"Isla," Gray said, unsure exactly what he wanted to say, but she walked without hesitation up the steps and across the landing into another door. He wondered if she had been here before at some stage. He followed, but she had already disappeared. He walked slowly down to the library to find the minister scratching at his desk. As he settled into a chair with a book, Beth appeared and climbed into the other one. There were times that they read together, but now she sat and watched him. He tried to ignore her, but she sat on the edge of the seat, focused solely on him.

"Leave him be," the minister murmured.

Beth continued her stare.

"You heard him," Gray mumbled.

"I don't want you to leave," she said.

"And where would I go?"

"Where she needs you."

"I don't think she does," Gray said, staring unseeing at the page.

Dinner passed in a blur. Gray was only half listening to the conversation, in which Calder barely grunted while Isla explained as much as she could of what she thought was going on. The minister nodded, and Beth moved her chair closer to Gray. They hadn't sat together at the table, and she had barely raised her eyes to him. He wondered if Alice would make an appearance, but he doubted it. There were more secrets than she had told him. She knew what her place was in the world, even if he didn't.

He only really started to pay attention when Beth was so close she was nearly sitting on his lap. He looked at her as she grinned up at him, and then the minster cleared his throat.

"I know," she murmured. "I want Gray to read me something."

"You can read it just as well," the minister chastised.

"Better, most likely," Gray mumbled. Something silver flashed in her eye. "No," he murmured.

She produced a book from he wasn't sure where and sat it down too loudly on the table. Isla looked across at it, and Calder straightened. Gray glanced at the child beside him and shook his head. He could read well enough, but he rarely did so out loud. Only on occasion in the class and with the other children.

"Bedtime story," Calder quipped. Gray didn't lift his eyes from the book other than to slide it back towards the child.

"Please," she pleaded.

"Beth," the minister said, his voice calm and cool. The smile slipped from the girl's face. "Another time." She took the book, patted Gray's arm and left the table. The other children were not far behind.

"I apologise for the child," the minister said. "She is keen on her study, and to help her fellow students."

"I bet she is ahead of you, E'anah," Calder continued.

"They are on equal footing," the minister said, his voice even as though answering an everyday query. "She has different gifts. Colonel, you will not wander beyond where you have been allowed to visit."

Calder bowed his head and pushed his chair back.

"Gray, I will talk with you later. Island and I have much to discuss."

Gray did the same as Calder, pushing his chair back. He bowed his head to the minister and, without glancing at Isla, he left the room. He heard Calder in the hallway behind him but moved straight to the library. Although he spent as much time with a book in his hand as he had before, he now spent more time in the classroom.

The lamp was on, and a soft glow filled the room. Beth was curled in a chair, the same book in her hand. Alice was in the opposite chair. Gray stopped, but Beth beckoned him forward and stood. He sat down and she climbed onto his lap, curling like Reilly's son had when he was small. She was much older, and yet she seemed small, fitting easily into his arms as she held the book out.

"I don't know why you do this," he mumbled.

"Because I love the sound of your voice," she whispered, opening the pages to where she wanted him to read from and handing it back.

"You have heard this a hundred times already."

"Indulge the child," Alice said, her focus on a book in her lap. "She won't have you much longer."

He was sure Isla would leave without him again. But someone always knew more than he did. Especially here. He indulged the child, lifting the book into the light and reading aloud from the pages. The image played out before them, and she squealed and clapped with delight as the story went on. The Rohen moved through the world as though they stepped through the room. It was a story she knew well, and although Gray was learning the history, he was amazed at how his words literally brought it to life.

He was still reading aloud quietly, taking in the soft snores of the child, when he realised Alice was gone and heard a sharp intake of breath behind him. He stopped, and the images faded as he took in Isla standing at the door. He closed the book, bundled up the child and she was gone.

Gray carried the child down to her room where Alice was waiting to get her into bed. He brushed her blonde hair back from her face, and for a moment she looked very much like Alice. He left her to it and headed for his own small room further down the corridor from the library. Not that he had used it as often as he could have, more often than not sleeping in the chair in the library. It had taken him days after arriving to begin using it.

He closed the door behind him, sitting on the edge of the bed in the dark to unlace his shoes. Something else he did far too often. He lay down and then sat straight back up. "Lights," he said.

Isla lay along this narrow bed, her arms along her side, her bare feet pointed. She looked scared or worried.

He stood up. She remained where she was, but she didn't look comfortable. It almost seemed like she was waiting for him to throw her out, or... she had been waiting in the dark. He sat down quickly and reached for her, but she flinched. He pulled his hands back in. She had seen what he could do, or at least what he appeared to do. He still wasn't sure himself that the skill was his, more likely the books themselves and their strange language.

"Why were you in the dark?" he asked.

"It doesn't worry me anymore."

"You look worried," he said, clenching his hands tighter together in his lap in fear of what they might do. Isla looked tired. "Did you get a room?"

She sat up then, swung her legs around and shuffled forward as though to stand. He took her hand. She stopped, her feet on the floor, seated on the edge of the bed with her eyes down. She didn't even seem to recognise his hand in hers.

"I'm sorry," he said, pulling back, and she squeezed it. "It is strange."

"You are just the same," she whispered without looking up.

"You don't look like you believe that," he said.

She swung around and crossed her legs, his hand still in hers. "I'm sorry," she said. "I missed you."

"You are sorry you missed me?" He wanted to sound playful, but his voice wasn't cooperating. "Or that you left me?" He bit his lip. He didn't blame her.

"I wanted to come back, but he wouldn't let me, and I knew the Rohen would help if they could."

"They did," Gray said. "I know."

"I had a task to do," she whispered.

He nodded, unsure that he could trust the words he wanted to say to come out right.

"Calder helped."

"Is he waiting?" As she scowled, he felt his face flush. He ran his fingers through his hair, brushing it out of his face and distracting his stupid mouth.

As he blew out a frustrated breath, she caught his hand and held them both. "I'm sorry," she murmured again.

"Stop. You don't have to be sorry. I'm the one being rude. You did what you had to do. I did as I was required. We can't always be..." He wasn't sure what they had to be.

"I didn't realise things would change so much."

"They haven't," he tried to reassure her, but he wasn't sure at what point they had. When she had gone, when she had returned. She was always so sure of herself. Now she was just where he needed her to be, and he was trying to push her away. He really needed a kick. Maybe he should have read the story at the table, but Calder came to mind again.

"No?" she asked, squeezing his hands. He nodded and then shook his head, unsure what he meant or if she was talking about Calder.

Kalli. He had been Kalli, and they had been alone—and he wasn't sure why it was killing him, but it was.

"Can I stay?" she asked.

"The minister is only too happy to…" He paused as she released her hold and stood. "You meant here?"

"It's ok, Gray. I was in a cage again, a small one, with the world crumbling around me. But you have work to do here."

"What cage?" he asked, standing while trying not to stand over her. The room was too small.

"Another facility—it doesn't matter." She tried to move around him, but he had her by the shoulders.

"Did he lock you up again?"

She shook her head, and he took her by the arm. She paused beside him as he stepped into the pathway between her and the door. "Isla, please stay."

She looked up then, uncertainty flashing across her face, and he was sure he saw more silver there in those intense green eyes than he had seen before. But he was seeing it everywhere, and he didn't release his hold on her. If she disappeared now, he might never find her again.

"I just need it to be like it was before."

"Of course," he murmured, pulling back the covers and nodding for her to climb in. He looked around, wondering if he should consider an alternative or sleeping on the floor, when she patted the bed beside her. He slipped in. She was warm and fluid as she lay alongside him, her head on his shoulder, and he shifted awkwardly to pull the arm out from between them and around her.

"I can sleep now," she whispered. He wondered then how long it had been. Had Calder dragged her around the universe, thinking she was helping him when he was supposed to be helping her? But Gray didn't ask. He knew anything else he asked would make him look stupid.

"How long have you been able to read Rohendra?" she asked, her voice soft, her breath brushing his chin, and he feared moving.

"Oh, feels like forever."

"Would you read to me?"

"Now?" He moved up to get out of the bed, but she wrapped her arms around him, her face buried in his chest. She didn't say anything, but he held her close, both arms wrapped tight around her. He could only hope that she wouldn't disappear by morning.

Eleven

I sla stared at the ceiling of the unfamiliar room and stretched. The bed was still warm, and yet it seemed strangely empty with Gray gone. She rolled over, pulled the blankets in around her and took in the child standing by the bed and staring at her. Her arms were crossed, her eyes narrowed.

"Where is Gray?" Isla asked.

"In the trees," the girl said, her fierce gaze still focused on Isla.

"Beth, isn't it?" Isla said, sitting up and reluctantly letting the blankets fall away. The child looked her over as though expecting something else within the bed. "We met yesterday. You know who I am."

"You will take him away," Beth said, her face hard. "I don't want you to take him away."

"It isn't up to me," Isla said.

"He would do anything you asked."

"Are you disappointed that he wouldn't read for you?"

"He did," Beth said, her features relaxing as though she remembered the joy of the images. Isla had never seen anything like it in her life. And she wasn't sure what it meant, for Gray or for her. "He always reads to me." The girl climbed up onto the bed beside Isla. "If you take him away, he won't be able to."

"You can read the words," Isla murmured, knowing it was true. There was a connection between all of the children here, some skill that had been lost.

"Not like Gray. I understand them, but I can't make them shine like he does."

It was an interesting term, and the memory of the glittering silver figures moving above the pages at the strength of his voice made Isla shiver. Despite his voice humming through her, she hadn't understood the words themselves.

"Can I learn?" she asked.

The child looked her over as though she might not have the skill, then shrugged and climbed back down from the bed. Isla scooped her hair back out of her face and wound it into a low bun, securing it with a tie she pulled from the Rohen around her.

Beth stood in the doorway waiting for her. Isla reached for her hand, and the child hesitated before she took it and led her out through the house. Isla had managed to find her own way the night before, but she really wasn't sure where she was going this morning. She had been so worried that Gray wouldn't forgive her for leaving him behind. Her relief had been overwhelming at seeing him safe. But there was something else about him, something she hadn't seen before, and she wasn't sure if it was the images or something else.

He wasn't happy that she had willingly gone with Calder. But she'd had to—it was what she had been instructed to do. He should have understood that. He was here doing his own thing.

Beth led her into the dining room, where several children moved slowly around the large man sitting at the table. The child at her side stopped.

"Good morning," Calder said, glancing up.

"Where is Gray?" she asked.

Calder pointed over his shoulder, and she looked out into the dense forest outside the window. As the child released her hold, Isla moved up to the glass and looked out. It was different from the forest she had grown up in. The trees seemed so much larger, so much closer together, and yet the light filtered through, the sun warming her through the window.

"Eat, and then you can explore," a soft voice said behind her, and she turned to take in the minister. The older man gave her a warm smile as he took his place at the head of the table.

"I'm not sure where I go next," she said, sitting down beside Beth in what had been Gray's seat the night before.

"I need to return to Rennet," Calder said through a mouthful of food. "The Hendra needs…" He looked back at his plate, and Isla wondered what he was going to say—that she needed him for support, or was he more worried for the child he thought was his?

She had tried to explain to him that it wasn't the case, that the Rohen would look out for their own. For she was fairly sure that was the case. The Rohen had protected her, or at least protected the child in some way. A daughter, a queen.

When she looked up from her plate, the minister was watching her closely. She wondered then at just who this man was, with his children and understanding of Rohendra. She had come here for a reason, willed herself far from where she was in the tight cage with Calder pressed against her and the building falling in around them. How many hummers had been lost?

She sipped at the hot tea in her hand, the familiar flavours comforting. At the silence around the table, she looked up. The minister was smiling, Calder was glaring and several of the children appeared in awe.

"Do that again," Beth begged.

Isla blinked, unsure what she could mean.

"Leave her alone; she needs some time," the minister murmured.

"Are they all hummers?" Calder asked, his voice cruel. She wondered why he had humoured her for as long as he had.

"We can send you back to Rennet," the minister said with a look of disappointment.

"They said he would help." Isla spoke as though she wanted him to stay, but she wasn't sure she did want that. And not if it meant she wouldn't see Gray. She looked beyond Calder to the forest through the window and wondered how far away he was.

"But he isn't," Beth said.

Isla looked down at the child staring across the table at the man eating as though he were starving. She was sure he had never gone hungry a day in his life.

"Maybe it isn't me he is meant to help," Isla whispered.

"We will learn the truth at some point," Beth said, slipping out of the chair and running from the room. The other children followed, and the minister stood slowly.

"Let me know what you wish," he said, but he was focused on Isla, not Calder. He bowed his head to her and followed the children.

"Is it just me or is it a bit strange around here?" Calder asked.

"It is you," Isla said, also standing from the table. She needed to find Gray.

She followed the idea of him through the forest, working her way between the trees. Although she sensed that many came this way on a regular basis, he had followed a different path. She wondered if the place she had led him to through the trees the day before was where he had gone. She closed her eyes and ran her hands over the trunks, allowing the threads of Rohen to lead her to him.

She heard him before she saw him, sounding frustrated, murmuring away in a language she didn't understand. The world shone silver around him. She stopped just beyond the trees, watching, hoping that he hadn't seen her and would continue whatever it was he was doing.

In some ways, it was similar to when he had read from the book, but his words weren't as clear. The images that danced around him were not nearly as clear as they had been, although they were larger, almost life size—at least compared to Gray.

He blew out a slow breath and the image disappeared.

"What are you doing?" Isla asked, and he jumped in surprise. "Sorry," she added.

"I thought you would be sleeping. You looked like you hadn't in some time."

She shook her head, unsure what she needed to tell him, why she needed to be sure they could work together.

"Breakfast will be served soon," he went on, looking back to the small clearing and where the figures had walked through not so long ago.

"I've eaten, and I doubt Calder would leave you anything."

He shrugged as though it wasn't important.

"Gray," she said, and when he focused on her she wasn't sure what she needed to tell him.

"Are you leaving?" he asked, his voice soft. He sounded somewhat hurt.

"Would you come with me?"

"So that is a yes."

"No, it is 'If I go, would you come too?'"

"I don't know that you need me. I'm not sure if I'm needed here, but I need to work out what I have."

She nodded then, fully understanding what it was like to want to understand her own skills. He could bring the words to life from the page—and almost from memory, it seemed. "Are you telling a story or remembering what you have read?"

"A mix of the two, but it doesn't seem to work."

"Have you spoken it before?"

He nodded, looking away from her.

"The same effect?"

"No," he said.

"Gray," she tried again, stepping closer, and for a moment it appeared as though he would step back. "I..."

"I understand," he said, turning his back to her. Something silver flashed again as he started to murmur.

When she stepped forward and put her hand to his arm, the image faded, but she wondered then if she should have waited. It looked different. Unlike what he had conjured from the pages of the book the night before, this looked familiar.

"Do that again," she said.

"I'm not sure I can."

"It looked like I knew it."

"A fight," he murmured. And then he looked at her as though seeing her for the first time. He turned sharply and rested his hands on her shoulders. "A fight," he repeated.

"You couldn't see the other side?" she asked. Something desperate made her heart beat fast, and a sick feeling welled up inside her.

"Maybe I need to reread it."

"You've seen it before?"

He nodded, but his brows creased as though he struggled to remember exactly. How many battles had there been? He started to murmur again, his voice a low whisper, his eyes closed as though he was trying to remember the story. The images flickered in the morning sunlight filtering through the trees, and then they were gone.

Gray had her by the hand, pulling her through the trees back to the house. He was confident in the path he followed, and Isla thought she must have been mistaken with him not having come this way before. He tugged her along the hallways. A child stepped back out of the way at one point, almost disappearing into the wall. And then they were standing in the library.

He let her go and moved straight to the shelves, running his fingers over the spines of the books, looking for something specific. It took her a moment to realise the minister was in the room, leaning over pages and scratching out the same odd symbols. He didn't even look up as Gray muttered something, and she was sure one book hummed a little louder than the others. Then Gray's hand closed around it and pulled it from the shelf.

He sat heavily in one of the chairs and, although not invited, Isla sat in the other. Gray flipped carefully through pages, his eyes running over them. Then he stopped, took a deep breath and began to read. The minister turned slowly in his seat as Isla moved to the edge of hers.

The figures moving through the room were Rohen, clearly the shimmering silver beings she had met beneath the surface of Urgway. Their arms were fashioned into swords, sharp and slender, and Isla shivered. She knew this—she had seen this. She had run into the middle of this very fight. It wasn't dark, and the light didn't flash off the blades as it did in her memories, but it was the fight she had been in.

She could see the faces of the unit she had belonged to, exactly as they had been, just as clear within the room as they would have been in the dark that night. The dusters pulsed; the blades moved swiftly. Isla focused on herself standing in the middle of the mayhem. Her eyes scared, her hand rose with a duster, but it didn't fire. The blades flashed around her. The sound of them moving through flesh frightened her like she couldn't remember ever being frightened in her life.

But they weren't attacking her. They worked around her. She was cut—she felt every slice through her skin, again and again, like she relived it—but it was only as they tried to kill others, tried to defend themselves.

Then she was falling and screaming, and as the image faded, she saw Kalli's face amongst the dead.

Gray took a deep breath and brushed at the tear that threatened to run down his cheek. He had felt the words unfold like they had in the room, and although he was well aware of Isla watching, he had kept his eyes on the page to ensure the words were correct.

As the image faded, she stood. Fear ebbed from her as she relived the fight that had impacted so much of her life. But there was something like relief in her face as he closed the book and looked up at her.

"They didn't try to kill me," she whispered, her eyes on the empty space at the centre of the small room where the scene had played out. "They knew what I was."

"And that is why they know you will help them," the minister said, standing and stepping up to take her hands. Had he entered during the scene? Or had he been here already when Gray had been too focused on the story to see him? Gray needed to know for himself what they were. He had seen glimpses before, but he knew her story was here. He ran his hand over the cover of the book again. A comforting hum passed through him, but it looked old and worn, well read, as though it had been in the library for a long time.

He glanced at the minister's desk, and when he looked back the man was smiling at him.

"We all have a task in this world. Ours are linked."

"You write the words and I read them."

The minister bowed his head, and Gray knew he wasn't alone in that. Alice had a skill in her ability to read the Rohendra, although he had not seen her bring the stories to life from the page. And there was something preventing him from saying aloud that she was here. There was a reason to keep it secret. Although he didn't know what it was, other than others were looking for her, it was something Calder could never know.

"He was there," Isla whispered, still staring at the floor.

Gray nodded. He had felt Kalli fall as the words had flowed through his mind, and yet he hadn't been there in the end. He might have been listed amongst the dead, but somehow he had survived that day—although not as Isla had. He was sure that Hendra was involved.

"You knew he died that day," Gray said.

Isla looked at him as though just realising he was in the room with her. She shook her head. "He swears he was not there. He was changing into what he is now."

"He might have changed because of what happened." Gray was tempted to again read the words that would bring his face into focus, and yet he knew with certainty who it was. He didn't want to do that to Isla again.

"How?" she asked.

"Sit down," the minister said quietly, gently applying pressure to her arm. Isla sat heavily in the chair. He waved towards the door, and a child appeared, the older girl who would bring him his tea. She nodded once and disappeared before he could ask, although Gray was aware that Isla could conjure her own tea.

"Will you tell me why you write what you do?" he asked the minister, and they both looked in his direction.

"Not how? You wish to know why?"

Gray nodded his head. There were many skills the peoples of the Rohendra Complex had that he was far from understanding, including his own. Many of them he was sure were connected to the Rohen, to the hummers. Although he wasn't one, he had a skill. He would never understand how it worked. But he wanted to know why this man had dedicated his life to writing the history, the stories of the Rohendra.

"It is what I am," he said with the same comfortable smile. "It is what I have always been."

"The children are gifted," Isla whispered.

The minister nodded and patted her arm as the girl reappeared with a tray, which she sat on the table before disappearing again. Gray leaned forward and poured tea into a cup, then handed it to Isla. Her hands shook a little, and he slipped to his knees to hold her fingers around the cup.

"They didn't try to kill me," she said again, her eyes on the cup. Gray was tempted to lift it to her lips, as she had for him when he wasn't able to help himself. But she wasn't injured.

"They would not harm you intentionally," the minister said.

"That is why I was saved, because I wasn't as dead as the others. It was accidental. They killed me accidentally."

Gray opened his mouth and then closed it, unsure how to respond. In some way, they had saved her, but it might take her some time to come to that conclusion. "Drink the tea," he coaxed.

She nodded but made no move to bring the cup to her lips.

"There is more for you to do," the minister said, standing straighter. With a glance at his desk, he left the room and pulled the door closed behind him. Gray wondered if the man knew the words to write the same way he knew what they were as he read them. Gray took the cup from Isla's hand and sat it untouched on the tray. When he turned back to her, she slipped from the chair to the floor beside him and wrapped her arms around him.

"I'm sorry he's gone," Gray murmured, holding her close. He had wanted to help in some way, yet it had only distressed her further.

"He's not," she said. "He's roaming the halls of this very building."

"That's not Kalli," Gray said, trying not to sound as angry as the idea made him. "He became something very different."

"It is him—I've seen it."

Gray pushed out of her hold and stood. He wanted to pace. He was too confused by Calder. The man was cruel, and his friend would never have been. There was more to him than Kalli, more than what had happened that day when he was cut down by the Rohen.

"He told me he wasn't there," she said. "He is so sure he wasn't there."

"He believed the lies and false memories then. He believed what you couldn't."

"I believed that for a very long time," she said. Was she trying to justify what this man had become?

"But it wasn't right. You knew it wasn't right."

She nodded and looked down into her lap, leaning against the chair. "Do the books tell you what we do next?" she asked after what seemed like too long.

Gray glanced over the shelves, but shook his head. There was a story here, their history. He understood them somewhat better than he had before, but it wasn't everything. "That's not what I'm here for."

"You are here for a reason," she said, slowly climbing to her feet. He wanted to step forward and ensure she was steady, but something held him back. "You are here to learn. But whatever comes next..."

He watched her. It was like he was waiting for her to tell him this was it, that they wouldn't see each other again and she couldn't find the words. It wasn't what they were, it didn't matter if they went their separate ways—and yet the idea of being separated again hurt. He had caused that hurt, and he was the reason she would leave with Calder, believing him still Kalli.

She blew out a long breath, and he steeled himself for the inevitable. "Just say it," he snapped, then bit down on his lip.

"I'm lost, Gray," she said. "Without you, it doesn't make sense."

"What?" he asked, his voice far too loud. She wasn't saying what he expected, and he didn't understand.

"I can't do this without you. The Rohen seems to think we have separate tasks, but they always lead back to each other."

"I'm not sure what you are saying," he mumbled, sitting back in the chair.

"You don't want to come," she said, looking at the space that had been filled with Rohen recently. He was tempted to pull a book from the shelves that would give her something of hope, but as he glanced back at the shelves, he wasn't sure.

"I do." He stood then, certain there would be something in the history covering the walls to help them both.

His hand rested on the first book, the one Alice had found for him that had opened his eyes to the world beyond what he had understood. He was sitting on the floor beside her, the book open in his lap before he could think too much about what he was sharing. They would understand. They had given him this gift for a reason, and they knew what he needed to do with her—what he needed to support her—because no matter what either of them thought, this had always been about Isla.

The worlds flowed easily, filling the room with the Rohen and the world they lived in. As he read, she watched, sometimes making noises of wonder or surprise and snuggling up into his side.

Gray was easily lost as the words washed over him. He didn't fully understand how Alice had helped him learn this. When he looked up from the page, the room had grown darker although someone had lit a candle. He wondered then at the papers on the minister's desk and the risk of the flame. The man hadn't returned. Isla was sound asleep, her head resting on his lap, and Calder stood in the doorway.

He glared, but there was something else, something almost like fear that made Gray wonder if there was still a hint of memory of the attack. Would he believe the images if Gray was to read from those pages for him?

Gray wanted to stand up to meet him but couldn't disturb the sleeping woman. Instead, he waved Calder into the room, and the broad soldier waited too long before he finally nodded. But he didn't move.

"Would you like me to read to you?" Gray asked.

"As though I were a child?" Calder snapped. Gray rested his hand on Isla's shoulder to remind the man that she was there. He stepped forward and sat in the soft chair, moving his feet around the sleeping Isla who pulled her legs up. She curled into a ball as though she knew he was there.

When Gray looked up, Alice hovered in the doorway. But within a heartbeat she was gone, and when Calder followed his gaze and turned to the doorway, it was empty.

"What would you read?" he asked, and Gray took a moment to realise the man was talking to him. "You have a book. What did you read to Isla?" he asked, indicating the woman at Gray's feet.

"The history of the Rohendra," he said, looking at the book in his hand.

"I won't understand it."

"It is in a form that everyone can understand," Gray said, still looking at the book. Was this something he should share with this man—would it help? They were so sure that he would help. At least, Isla was sure. Although Gray thought what he had managed to do so far wasn't enough. Had they done as they needed to, or had it all been lost when Isla pulled them here?

"I'm not sure I need the history."

"What happened the day she nearly died?" Gray asked, wondering just what this man did know. What he remembered.

Calder sighed and, leaning back in the chair, closed his eyes. It was the first time Gray had seen him truly expose himself, for Gray could take him in that moment. "I thought there was a chance."

"She thought you were lost that day."

"I was never there, but to her I was lost."

"Not that you were ever truly mine," Isla whispered. Gray rested his hand back on her shoulder. She tapped the book that sat on the floor before him, and he realised he hadn't returned it to the shelves. "The history might be good for him."

"Where should I start?" Gray asked, his heart beating fast, unsure what reaction this would get from Calder.

"Near the end," she whispered.

Calder sighed again and sat forward, but his gaze was on Isla, who hadn't moved. He nodded once.

Gray ran his finger over the page. The images appeared so clear for him as he looked down at Isla, who smiled up at him. He began to read. Calder sat forward in his seat as the battle raged around the woman standing, scared and still and silent, in the middle of the mess as stray swords sliced into her. And as she fell, and the sadness of the Rohen was palpable in the room, Isla shuddered. The faces of the fallen became clear and, as Kalli's face appeared, Gray stopped reading. It hovered in the air for only a moment before it was gone.

He was on his feet then as Isla moved closer to Gray. "You did that?" he asked, something accusing and yet worried at the same time. "You made that look like he was there."

Gray blinked up at the man, not at the idea that he thought it was a lie but at the separation he put between himself and the man he used to be.

"That was you," Isla said.

Calder shook his head.

"Yes," she said, making to stand, but Gray took her arm and stopped the motion.

"I have to return. There is nothing I can do that will assist you. And there is nothing you can do that will help me." He turned for the door, and Gray wondered how far away Alice was. Would she show herself to Isla if Calder were to leave?

Maybe he needed more time to learn what he was and how he could help.

"The minister can show you the way," Gray offered. "Although you won't know where we are."

"Draroh," Calder murmured. "I don't care what you are up to, E'anah. You are not nearly as important as you think you are." He looked back to where the images had shown him who he used to be.

"Goodbye, Ka... Colonel," Isla said, half risen from the floor, her hand on Gray's knee to keep her balance.

He bowed his head in a surprise show of respect, and the minister was waiting when he turned. Calder bowed his head to the older man and followed him along the hallway. Gray wondered how he would find the travel back to Rennet and whether the Rohen would take him to exactly where he needed to go.

"I told you he wasn't Kalli," he whispered.

"Someone thinks he is."

Twelve

Hendra stepped back against the desk as Calder appeared in the middle of her office. She might have actually squealed with surprise. He looked at her as though not quite seeing her and then around the room. He blinked, staggered a couple steps and then stood to attention.

"How?" she stammered. "Where have you been?" She hoped her voice sounded more level and together than she thought it did.

"Trying to stop an uprising," he mumbled.

"I don't think you've succeeded."

"What?"

Hendra moved around the desk, using it to lean against as she found her chair and sat down. She was more shaken than she thought she could be, half waiting for the hummer to appear behind Calder as she had the last time he'd arrived in her office.

"Are you unwell?" he asked, racing forward. She held up her hand, stopping him mid-step.

"I'm fine. But you were looking at facilities and then you were gone. And my store appears to have been blown up. Last I saw, you were chasing after that girl. How far did you go?"

"Draroh," he murmured, then looked at her as though he hadn't meant to tell her.

She sighed. "Was she behind this?"

He shook his head.

"Any sign of Alice?"

He shook his head again. There was a hesitation in him that she hadn't really seen before. As though he held secrets. She didn't like that idea.

"Is she coming back?" Hendra asked.

"Who?" he asked too quickly, and she wondered who he had been thinking of.

"The hummer."

"Did you know?" he asked, stepping forward.

There was something haunting in the way he looked at her, something possibly angry. She had seen him mad before, but he had never aimed that anger at her. For the first time, Hendra wondered what he might have learnt and what that might mean for her. He was her greatest weapon, but there was no way he could learn the truth of what had happened. He had wanted this. She wasn't confident of how he might react if he learnt the truth of how she had made it happen.

"What exactly do you think I know?" she asked, dreading the answer.

"How Kalli died."

She paused, surprised in a way that he thought of the man as someone different from himself. "Everyone knows the story of how he died," she said. "That was the point, that Island Tarle could be the only survivor. Although maybe if you had both survived, it might have been something very different."

"How did you manage that?"

"Sorry?"

"How did you make it look like I died with the rest of the unit while I was off having this done?" he asked, indicating his face. His voice was low and slow, as though she might not understand the question.

"We'd planned this," she reminded him. It had been planned for some time later, but it had become necessary to do it then—the loss had made it necessary. How the doctors had managed it, she didn't know, and she had made certain those involved couldn't share the secret. No one knew who he was or what he had been before she had him inserted into another unit, and before long he was running it. Without disruption to the Complex, her Calder had replaced the former soldier.

He shook his head, but not as though he didn't believe her—as though to shake an image away.

"Where have you been?" she asked again. "What did she try to tell you?"

"That I was there. That Kalli was there."

"She had to believe that to believe the lie. You would have led them in if you had been there; that is what was on the recording. How much does she remember of the truth?"

"Enough," he murmured, his eyes glazed and staring into the distance. There was more that he wasn't telling her.

"You believe her," she said. "Over me, you believe the hummer. She is confused between what did happen and what she was told."

"I saw it," he whispered, something she had never seen before in his face. Was it fear? True fear?

"How?"

"E'anah," he muttered, turning for the door.

"Calder," she called after him. He stopped but didn't turn back. "Where were you?"

"I don't know. Somewhere with children, somewhere deep in the forest. I couldn't find it again," he said, turning slowly, "even if I tried. I'm not even sure what he did to get me here."

"The enforcer?"

"The minister."

Hendra stood up and leaned forward.

"I don't know how to find it," he repeated.

"I do," she whispered. Or at least she had an idea, although the property was remote. Unless someone wanted her there, she wouldn't be able to reach it.

"What is it?" he asked, stepping forward.

"Alice," she breathed.

He shook his head.

"She was there," Hendra said. She knew it in her bones. Alice was still helping them. "Tell me how you got there," she demanded, hurrying around the desk.

"I was taken by Isla. The building was collapsing, and then we were in a forest."

"Where was the building?"

"Oric," he said.

"You are certain of that?"

"It was my facility. I know what planet I was on."

"But then you were on Draroh?"

"Yes!" he bellowed. The door opened, and a secretary's worried face appeared. Hendra waved him away, and he glanced at Calder before closing the door.

"That was Alice's home," she explained, exasperated that he didn't know that. Shouldn't he know that? He was supposed to be looking for Alice, but then he'd gone off with the hummer, following her around the universe after she wasn't sure what. Why had she allowed that to happen?

"Alice is dead—or gone."

"You and the hummer assured me she wasn't dead. She has therefore run away. And she has likely run home. If you could reappear in this office in an instant, then she could have made the reverse trip the same way."

He shook his head.

"How?"

"I don't know!" he said, striding forward. "I was in the house, and then I was blindfolded so as not to show the way, and before I had the chance to take a breath—the cold rushing over me—the blindfold had disappeared and I was standing in your office."

"What?"

He opened his mouth and then closed it. Frustration marked his face, and she wondered if he would have lashed out at her, had she been anyone else.

"How did the hummer take you to Draroh?"

"We were trapped. She had squeezed her eyes closed and I was trying to shield her from the building, and she pulled away from me although there was nowhere to go. I held her too tight and we were in the trees." He took a ragged breath. "And then she was apologising for where she was—people, children, E'anah."

"She went to him," Hendra mused, wondering just what that meant.

"She didn't know he was there. She didn't even appear to know where we were at the time."

"I don't believe she didn't know, but I need to know how."

He shook his head, growling something under his breath, and then he was stomping out of the office. He used the main door, which was unusual for him, and he didn't even close it afterwards.

She stood for too long watching after him, and a secretary appeared and closed the door. She continued to stare, hoping in some way he would come back. What had he seen, where had he seen it and why did she feel there was far more to the story than he had explained? Why was he not going to take the time to tell her what that was?

In the distance, another explosion sounded. The building shuddered just a little, and she wondered if it was worth her moving to somewhere safer—although she wasn't sure where that might be. She rushed to the window to see if she could identify where the attack had occurred, but she wasn't sure. There was no real pattern to where the attacks were occurring, or at least that was how it appeared to her. But there didn't seem to be an end to them.

She stared at the lone whisp of smoke that made its way into the sky. At times there were several sites at once, but this was the only one currently burning. It was starting to look like there was a constant haze across the city.

"Hendra," a deep voice said behind her, too close. She tried not to flinch.

"General, are these attacks occurring on other parts of Rennet?"

"Across the whole Complex."

"In the trees?"

"I'm not sure I understand," he said.

She turned from the view and took him in, glancing over his shoulder at the still-open door. "Are the attacks only happening in built-up areas?"

"Mostly."

"The instigators?"

"We haven't been able to pin that down."

"Is there a theme amongst their targets?"

He shook his head. "Originally it was Hendra buildings, but now it is more random and sporadic."

"Showing the people that they can't be stopped, or at least that we can't stop them."

"It appears that way."

"And what are you doing about it?"

"We are having trouble tracking down any intelligence, any idea as to who is behind this."

"The Sparrow?"

"There aren't any of them left, and no connections that we can make. We have soldiers making their way through known hangouts of former troublemakers, but there is nothing. Either there is no sign of them or no sign that they were causing any trouble. There is something very unknown about this."

"That makes me very nervous," Hendra murmured, looking back towards the door.

"I heard the colonel has returned."

She nodded and moved back to her desk. She chewed on her lip as she sat down and then focused on the man standing before her.

"Don't you have rebels to find?"

"Did you get what you needed from the colonel?"

"Not exactly, no."

"The hummer—will she help?"

"She didn't return with him."

"He let her go?"

"She wasn't a prisoner, General. She was assisting with a project. And it appears that she let him go, not that he seems very happy with the idea. If you feel you can use him to assist with finding the rebels, I release him from any task he might have had for me."

"What might he be doing for you?" the general asked. Although his words were polite, she was surprised by the query.

They both turned at a knock at the open door, and Michaels stood there looking nervous.

"Thank you, General," she said politely, waving the scientist forward. "You know what you need to do."

He bowed his head and left, pausing at the door for too long before closing it behind him. Had everyone forgotten their place in the universe? She gave the directions—they followed them. No one was to question what those instructions were or what she might have given to others.

"Michaels, please take a seat," she said, indicating the table across the room. He moved somewhat nervously and then took a seat. As she walked closer, he stood again and bowed, but she waved him back down before she sat at the end of the table.

The man nervously cleared his throat.

"I understand that you were not responsible for the disappearance of the garden," she said. He seemed to breathe for the first time.

"I don't understand it," he stammered. "She assured me it was safe."

"The hummer?"

He opened his mouth and then closed it.

"Start at the beginning."

"We arrived at Urgway. They went out into the garden—"

"Both of them?" she interrupted.

He nodded. "In protective clothing, although they weren't wearing it when they came back. It was like..." He took a deep breath, and she waited while he seemed to work out how best to tell her what had happened. She had his report, quite soon after it had all occurred. But she needed to hear it from him, and she was sure there were things that had occurred on the base that she hadn't been told. "It was like they had been away somewhere. They looked exhausted, but they seemed confused about the amount of time they'd been gone. They came in through the wall," he whispered, leaning forward a little as though she wouldn't understand.

"The wall?"

"It just opened." He moved his hands in front of him like opening doors, wonder and awe written across his face. "They walked in as though nothing had happened, and it closed up behind them."

"Did you think she did that?"

He nodded and then shook his head. "It was almost like it—the wall—knew what she needed. She just walked towards it; it opened and then closed. She nearly did the same the following day, but I'm not sure she was herself then."

"Explain that," Hendra said carefully.

The man looked down at his hands, enthusiasm gone. "She wasn't quite the same the next morning, or was it that Gray wasn't the same..."

"You aren't really explaining this," Hendra said.

"He knew what she was." Michaels implored her to understand with his dark beady eyes. "He was trying to protect her, explaining things as though she were a child. She wasn't surprised the garden was gone, and she started to open the wall while we all stood there. She went out onto the sand where the garden had been, but it was like she wasn't really looking. Like she already knew where it was. And then Calder appeared. She walked back in through the wall again, and she was friendly. It was very confusing."

"I would imagine so," Hendra said softly.

"And then she appeared in the room."

"Appeared? Who did?"

"Island Tarle."

"When exactly?"

"Colonel Calder was interrogating them, although they weren't really telling him anything, and I appreciate that I wasn't supposed to be listening..." Hendra raised her eyebrows in surprise. "But she knew where it had gone, I just knew it, and she wasn't going to tell Calder anything. And then there was a second Island Tarle in the room, and Gray looked so relieved to see her, as though the other one wasn't really her."

Hendra pushed up from the table, a nervousness moving through her. Calder hadn't shared any of this. Instead, he had taken her far away—far away from Hendra—as though he were trying to protect her. As though he cared about her. And he hadn't even cared when he was pretending to be in a relationship with her. What had happened that he would put this woman's needs ahead of Hendra's?

"Then what happened?" she prompted, turning back to the nervous man at the table.

"She disappeared."

"Which one?"

"The one who wasn't her," he stammered, and although it didn't really make sense, it did. "She dissolved into a puddle of Rohen and disappeared into the floor."

"She left willingly?"

"Isla told her she wasn't needed."

Hendra let out a slow breath, not realising she had been holding it. Isla was working with the Rohen. She said she remembered, that she knew what they were. She clearly knew far more than Hendra had understood her to. And Calder was aware of all of it.

"What do you think happened?" she asked the man at the table.

"I think she manipulated the Rohen in some way. I think she hummed it." There was something excited about the way he spoke, something sparkling in his eyes—something he would like to experiment on, she thought. With the trouble around the Complex, he would have to wait. But it might be that the Rohen were far more involved than she'd first considered.

Thirteen

Isla looked up as Gray sat at one of the desks in the classroom, the children all around him. The minister had said she could observe from the back of the room, although she would likely understand very little.

There was a feeling of expectation as they waited. Even Gray seemed to watch the door. Then Alice strode through, all smiles, and took a seat at the desk. She glanced over the children, but her gaze didn't linger on Isla at all. Isla wondered how long she had been here. Had she just arrived, or had she been hiding from Calder?

Isla had a lot of questions, but she didn't think they would be answered today. In fact, she was confident that no matter who she asked, her questions would not be answered at all. Even by Gray.

Alice sat, opened a book and appeared to read silently to herself. The others in the room followed her example, opening whatever books they had before them to read. All except for Beth, who closed her eyes and sat still, her hands sitting one over the other on top of the book.

This was not like Isla's memory of a classroom. Although where she had grown up was somewhat different to what would be considered normal, these children didn't appear to be learning. When Beth made a small wincing noise, Gray looked across at her but didn't move. It was only when a boy just in front of Isla raised his hand that it seemed like a classroom.

Alice called him forward, and he sat the book before her as he whispered something. She moved her hand through the air, leaving a symbol shimmering in the light. "Who can describe this for Marca?"

They all looked up, and several children said something at once. The word they each pronounced sounded similar, but Isla wasn't sure. Despite the hours Gray had read to her, she couldn't make out anything familiar with the language. She might have seen the symbol before, but she couldn't be sure.

"Danger," Beth whispered.

"Gray?" Alice asked.

He said something, a word she couldn't have repeated, his voice low and deep, and an image appeared before the class. It was a man, an older man, but not one Isla recognised.

"Do you have a word for this?" Alice asked. When Isla refocused on her, she realised Alice was asking her.

She shook her head.

"Hendra," Gray said.

Alice nodded.

"All Hendra or just this one?" Isla asked.

"The words sound the same, and yet each Hendra is an individual. Gray, would you mind?" Alice asked, her voice sweet.

He said another word that sounded very much like the first, and the current Hendra appeared. Isla thought Alice might flinch at the sight of her, but she didn't.

"Queen," Beth murmured, her eyes still closed.

"Thank you, Beth," Alice said, although she looked a little annoyed.

"I've heard her called that before," Isla said. She wondered if the Rohen had been referring to the Hendra or the child she carried.

"Gray," Alice prompted.

Another word, one similar to the others. Isla was almost sure he was saying the same word, and yet a different image appeared. Another woman dressed in the royal blue of the Hendra, but she was not the woman Isla knew to be Hendra now. She was tall, slender, beautiful—something silver flashed around her eyes.

"Rohendra," Isla breathed.

"Life," Beth whispered, her eyes still closed. Gray reached across and took her hand. Despite having her eyes closed, she reached back in turn.

"How do you know these words?" Isla asked.

"We are taught," a child said. "But not everyone can learn."

Isla nodded.

"They are not hummers as you would know the term," Alice said. The idea had not occurred to Isla. She had thought of them as gifted. But then, hummer wasn't a term she thought of when it came to herself—although she had used it to describe herself, and she could feel the hum of the heartbeat of the universe and form what she needed from the Rohen.

"You have different skills," the boy continued. "Like the tea," he said with a grin.

"The universe is formed from Rohen," Alice said.

"I would like to understand more about it, particularly what the Rohen want from us."

"They tell us what they need," another child whispered, but his eyes were on the image of the unfamiliar woman standing at the front of the classroom. As Isla looked at her more closely, she saw something familiar about her. As though she knew her—could know her.

The image blinked and smiled again, and her eyes shimmered. She was certainly a child of the Rohendra. Isla wondered then how much of the Rohen threaded through the current family line. The current Hendra was determined to destroy them, even though she was sure her father knew what they were and had worked with them. She had changed so much, threatened so many. As the woman faded, Isla could only imagine the cold, hard bars of the cage she knew a hummer had been kept in. Despite her own fears she had experienced in the glass cage, it was nothing compared to what that would have been.

"Will you tell me how it was done?" she asked, but Alice shook her head ever so slightly. There was more she might be able to learn, but not in front of these children. "Will you teach me the history?"

Alice studied her as though she were asking for so much. But she had been tasked by the Rohen. She worked with them—for them—to learn what she could to assist them. To prevent the Hendra from causing more damage to them and the universe itself.

"Do you know what I am to do next?" she asked, wondering if her place now was to sit and watch Gray learn what he could. Would he become like the minister, working through the pages of history for someone else to bring to life?

"What would you do?" Alice asked as though she were a child with no purpose, finding her skills. Would she turn to healing? Would she...? Isla didn't know where she fit. Her confidence had been so strong, so sure of what she had to do, and now it was gone. Calder with it. Should she stay or go back into the Complex?

"Would they destroy it?" Isla was unsure where the words came from, but she knew there would be more losses. More damage at the hands of the Rohen to save the Complex.

"No," Alice whispered, her eyes closed. Isla was reminded of Tevia and wondered just how much the others were able to communicate with the Rohen. Her own time with them had been so limited. "You are useful. You will help our queen."

A whisper moved through the class, and Gray turned his dark eyes to study her with the children. Isla backed up, unsure when she had stood.

As Gray stepped towards her, she was out the door and running through the trees. She knew far more than she thought, and yet a few moments in a classroom had disrupted everything she'd thought she knew. She was sure she heard the master calling after her. She ran faster, working her way between the large trees, feeling the path, her hand on the bark where others had travelled before her—and then there was nothing, no idea of anyone else but the trees, and the warm air wrapped around her and the sweat on her skin. She ran until there was nothing left, no breath left in her lungs to move her forward, and she looked up at the shimmering figure before her.

A moment of fear washed over her, and then she remembered the image from the night before—the blades moving around her, her own inactivity. The slices through her body had been accidental. And then the image of Kalli and his vacant stare returned, and she shuddered.

"You are what you are," the deep voice whispered over her skin, vibrating through her body as though it were the hum of the universe.

"Is it enough?"

"You are more than enough. You are a child of the Rohendra."

"Me?" she asked.

"Gifted means different things to so many. The master knew what you were."

"An orphan," she sighed.

"You are never alone in the forest," he whispered. Isla felt the comfort of the words, the familiarity of their meaning and that they weren't just words.

"I don't remember my parents," she said, looking at the man before her. "Were they the reason I was gifted?"

"You have always known your origins, child."

Isla sighed. She wouldn't learn the truth from them, only parts of it. Despite her willingness to help, for she understood that she had to, she couldn't see a way forward. She had stopped the containment; the Rohen trapped by the Hendra was free. But there was more to this than that, and despite what she might have tried to tell the Hendra, the woman was determined to remove the Rohen from the Complex. She would destroy them all.

"How do I convince her? She will reopen the mines, won't she?"

"That was her plan," he said. "She thought she would learn to control us, but she hasn't."

"The Rohen is the Complex," Isla said. A fear shuddered through her, that the Hendra might deliberately destroy them all just to remove the Rohen. Only she would never be able to achieve that. "You know what is coming," she said, thinking of the young woman in the Hendra uniform. The feeling of knowing her increased every time she recalled her. She shook her head, trying to dispel the odd thoughts.

"We have seen what is to come. You knew this, for you were told."

"But I don't understand. Alice poisoned her; she could have harmed the child."

"She helped the child, gave her what was needed to ensure she is strong. Alice is a carer."

Isla nodded. It made sense—the healing, the watching over the Hendra until she was pregnant, ensuring the child was what she needed to be. And now she watched over these children. More gifted, sharing the world of the Rohen or sharing the world with the Rohen?

"Would it not be easier if the worlds knew what you were?"

"We are as we should be. You are as you are."

Isla sighed, unsure how to proceed. Would she have to convince the Hendra to save them all by pretending they didn't exist? Focus on her own child, the one who would heal what the Hendra started.

"You have to tell me what I am to do next," she said, hoping she didn't sound as desperate as she felt. "I don't know where to go. I don't know what to do. I need a task, a mission—I need something that only I can do."

"Save Kalli," he said.

"It is too late," she whispered, remembering him again as a corpse on the ground amongst the many others of that day. "He's gone. Calder said so himself."

"Calder can't remember how he was made. Remind him."

Isla wanted to scream that she would take any other task, but she bit down on her lip as she heard footsteps moving quickly behind her. The silver being before her disappeared.

"Isla?" Gray huffed as he appeared between the trees.

"He will lead you to the right path," a deep voice vibrated through her.

"They don't mean me," Gray said. She shook her head. She didn't want this—she didn't want to be anywhere near Calder at this time. And how he could help her, she wasn't sure. He had said Kalli was dead. He felt he was something different, knew himself to be a different man, and yet he had stayed with her until the moment he had learnt he had been there.

"I don't want this," she whispered.

"There is very little choice around what we are required to do. We're at war, whether we want to be or not," Gray said, his voice low and measured. "We do as we are directed."

"Have you seen what is to come?"

He gave her a sad smile rather than an answer, and she feared pushing him would give her what she didn't want to know. He had told her that he couldn't see it, yet he had a word for the next Hendra, a woman Isla knew although she hadn't been born.

"What does Alice think?"

"Why?"

"You listen to her. You appreciate her counsel."

He looked back through the trees. "She helped me find what I am. What I can do to help."

"Can you help me?"

"That is my purpose." He bowed his head, and Isla was flooded with relief. She threw her arms around his neck and was relieved when he closed his arms around her and held her tight.

"Is there a Rohendra word for Calder?"

He let her go, and she stepped back. Then he shook his head.

"They seemed so sure he would help."

"Kalli," he whispered. The man she had known reappeared before her, real enough that she could have touched him. Something sharp cut through her chest, and then he was gone.

"We have to find him," she said. "We have to find a way to use him against Hendra."

"Against Hendra?"

"Ok, we have to find a way to stop Hendra, and Kalli is the way."

"He isn't Kalli anymore," Gray said.

"There are those who think he is—but what that is, I don't know."

Calder paced the small room. It felt like an age since he had been here. It had just been a room, never a refuge, and yet he felt the need to hide. He tried to calm his breathing, steady the shake that seemed to take hold of his body. He closed his eyes and then instantly opened them again as the image of his own face lying among the dead returned.

Isla had been so sure he had been there, but no matter what he tried, he couldn't remember that. It was something to distract from the fact that he hadn't been there. Something Gray had concocted.

But he knew that wasn't true. He wouldn't have hurt Isla with a false image if it weren't what had happened. He was amazed then at just what skill the man had. There had never been a hint of it when they were children or on the Sparrow.

He closed his eyes, took a deep breath and remembered Gray sitting on the floor, the book in his hand, Isla sleeping or at least resting across his lap. Had she done that with him? In the sun perhaps, but he didn't think so. He had wanted to be close to her, and yet he couldn't allow himself to become attached. In many ways, it was as the recording had stated, and yet it wasn't. They were deep underground, yet there were trees—odd trees. Was that the problem? Was that why she wouldn't fight?

They were to destroy what was Rohen—the trees, the odd plants—and Isla had refused. It scared her, and he couldn't remember her being afraid. Not then. He had seen it too many times since he had re-entered her life. Since Hendra had sent him back in to find and destroy her. Did she fear what she would remember? Hendra had needed a hero, something to distract from the horror of what had happened and what she had done.

He rubbed at his face and ran his fingers back through his short hair. It didn't make any sense that Hendra would lie to him, despite his understanding that she lied to nearly everyone else. But she had her reasons. What reason did she have to lie to him? That she had sent him in, had him killed along with everyone else and then somehow pulled him from the carnage and remoulded him as she needed him to be?

This was who he was—this was who he had always been. But he had cared for Isla. There were moments when it was just the two of them, alone and away from the others. She was still the soldier, and yet she was more than that. He had always known she was more than anyone else understood her to be.

In that moment in the cage, sure the world would collapse on them, he'd wanted only to hold her and yet she'd pulled away from him. Then to watch her sleeping, comfortable and relaxed for the first time in so long against

Gray as he read from his strange books... it hurt that she couldn't feel that way with him.

Calder stomped out of the small room, down the corridor through the silent building and out into the sunshine. The world smelt of smoke and, although he couldn't see any at the moment, he knew more bombings were coming. It was what he was designed for—war. Hendra had ensured that. And yet he still wanted to be with Isla. He tried to shake the idea away.

Hendra had done so much for him, had cared for him, and he would do anything for her in return. He worried about her and her child—their child, he was sure, although Isla didn't believe that either. She should never have guessed that he thought it his. What had she seen? What had he done that might put the Hendra in danger?

He looked back at the building standing tall against the skyline and wondered how he had made it so far. His mind wasn't his own, and he had to find a way to focus on what was important. But then, he wasn't sure what that was. He knew she had lied to him, taken from him—for the good of the Complex, she would have told herself. But whether he could believe that, he was no longer sure.

A troupe of soldiers jogged past, each saluting as they went. He bowed his head but didn't salute in return. He didn't have it in him. He needed instructions, needed a focus.

Fourteen

G ray wanted desperately to take one of the volumes with him, but he didn't know which one. As he brushed his hands over the spines of the books, he knew he couldn't take them from the building. They belonged here—they were needed here—and it would hurt to take them. He tried not to sigh.

"I'm sorry," a soft voice said behind him as Isla's arms closed around him and she rested her head against his back. "Is it hard to leave?"

"No," he said honestly, "but it is hard to leave the words I've come to understand."

"You can always bring them with you."

"I…" He unclasped her hands at his waist and turned around. She smiled sadly up at him as though she understood, and yet he wondered if anyone truly understood what he was parting with. "I can't take them."

"You know them," she said, running her fingers along the side of his face. "No one can take the words from you. It is your language as much as theirs."

He shook his head, unsure if that was true. He understood the words on the page. He could read aloud. He could read to himself.

"What is the Rohendra word for me?"

He looked at her then, wondering what she meant. What she thought it could do to help him.

"Does it translate to Island? Or dragonfly?"

The word formed easily in his mind. He had spoken it amongst others when he was reading, but he hadn't said it by itself. He pressed his lips closed, unsure what it would mean if he said the word aloud. What if she was disappointed? But it was as though it pushed from his lips, needing to be spoken whether he was willing or not.

An image of her appeared in the middle of the room. It was a shimmering copy of her as she was now. Whisps of her hair free from the braid, a sprinkle of freckles across her face, a confidence in the way she stood. He looked at the real woman studying the image. The confidence appeared to have slipped of late. He wanted to help her regain that, but he knew it was there inside her somewhere. Both women smiled at him as the shimmering version disappeared.

"That is how you see me," she said.

"That is what you are," he replied. "It is not my word."

"Tell me what it would be in common tongue."

"The Dragonfly," he whispered.

"Dragonfly," she murmured. Was she disappointed?

He shook his head. "*The* Dragonfly."

"So a dragonfly is different."

He muttered a word that, despite meaning almost the same, sounded very different even to his own ears. A silver image of a dragonfly zipped around the room, and she laughed. The sound warmed his very core. He whispered the word again and again, filling the room with silent movement.

She rose up on tiptoes to run her fingers through the silver images. Gray half expected them to fly around her, but they continued on their path around the room, ignorant of the woman's delight and attempts to catch them. She leapt for one, almost tripping over the small table between the chairs, and he pulled her close before she fell.

She closed her arms around his neck and kissed him as though it were the most natural thing in the world. He didn't pull away.

It was only at a soft cough by the door that he pulled back. "I thought you didn't have that kind of relationship," Alice said, her voice too loud and a little cruel.

Isla released him and stepped back, but he didn't let her step out of his reach. He pulled her close again. "It is what it is," he said, unable to keep the smile from his face.

"You sound more like a minister every day," Alice continued, entering the room. "I understand you are to leave."

He nodded, although he had no idea where they were to go or what they were to do.

"Are you fighting on the right side?" she asked.

"We are seeking balance," Isla said, still facing Gray rather than Alice, and he thought he saw a hint of her earlier confidence returning.

"Where will you seek it?" Alice asked. Isla turned to take her in.

"You know what must be done."

"As do you. And it will not be easy. It cannot be done with dusters and rifles."

"But it might be done with swords," Isla whispered, her body rigid, her voice level.

He might have seen what was, but she appeared more confident in what was to come. The Rohen, he reminded himself, seemed to know what was coming, what the Complex would be. Did they really have to fight so hard if they knew it would be theirs? Or was that why they knew it would be? He shook his head at the ideas racing around.

"Where would you have us go?" Isla asked.

"You will know where you are needed. My father is willing to send you to where you need to go—or shall you go yourself?" Alice asked, and again

Gray sensed a touch of something not like her usually confident self. She knew her place here, her place with the Rohen and her own skills.

"Do you want to return?" he asked.

She looked a little confused for a moment, then gave him a smile and shook her head. "My place is here."

"Is that not enough?" Isla asked, real curiosity in her voice. The woman at the door sighed.

"I want it to be," she replied.

"And then it will be."

As Alice closed the door behind her, Gray pulled Isla closer, slipping his hand around her jawline and behind her head. She tilted her head back up to him, and he kissed her. He closed his arms around her back, pulling her closer, holding her as though he may never get the chance again.

When their lips parted, she took a deep breath and smiled up at him, her arms still tight around him. He felt comfortable, as though he were where he was meant to be.

"Oh," she said.

"I wasn't sure I would get another chance. Not once we leave."

She shook her head, her brow furrowing a little as though she were trying to work out what came next.

"Where are we going?" he asked.

"Kalli," she whispered, leaning against his chest. He was disappointed that he couldn't see her face.

"This is what they want."

"It is what it is," she whispered.

Fifteen

Hendra looked at the men around the table and wondered if this was the right idea. She knew it was what needed to be done, but she wasn't sure these men were the ones to implement those plans. Michaels sat opposite her at the table, looking somewhat uncertain. The general sat beside him, busy watching the third man, Calder, as he continued to pace back and forth on the opposite side of the room by the windows.

"Something must be done to stop it. This is that something," she insisted.

Michaels made an odd sighing sound, and she glared at him across the table.

"I don't think this is a good idea," he said weakly. "There is far more to this metal than we understand. I have seen some strange things..."

"How long have you worked with it?" the general asked him.

"Most of my career, and yet it is in the last few weeks that I have seen so much more." There was a sense of awe to his words, and the general sat forward. Was he listening to this rubbish? She gave a subtle shake of her head, but the general wasn't watching her. Or he chose to ignore her. "The hummer," Michaels continued, "could do so much. And that wasn't just because of her connection to the Rohen—it was as though it listened and spoke with her. And then there was the copy."

"More perfect than the original," Calder muttered from across the room. Hendra glared at him, wondering what he knew and what else he hadn't shared with her.

"It talked like her. It was her, and yet it wasn't," Michaels said.

There was an odd, muffled laugh from across the room, and she glared at the back of the man now staring out the window.

"Rick?" the general asked. She wondered then why she had only ever used his last name. From his previous life, he'd only ever had one name, a family name perhaps.

He shook his head but continued staring out the window.

"General," she said, trying to keep her voice level, "I hope you don't think that this is not what I need."

He gave her an odd look, and she wondered if the words had made sense.

"I know what they are. I know the risk they pose to the Complex. The mines must be destroyed."

"There is more to the metal than the mines, and you will only cause more trouble, more angst." Michaels said, too confidently. What did he know?

"There will be more death," Calder muttered, turning from the widow.

"Theirs. The Rohen would destroy us all."

"Only if that were what was needed for the Complex."

"You are following the hummer now?" Hendra asked, allowing her anger to be heard. But he shook his head as he walked towards the table. He didn't take a seat, pacing behind the other two instead. She would rather he had stayed by the window. It was far less distracting.

"I am trying to do my job," he said. "The position you gave me—security, protection of you and the Complex. Doing this puts you in danger. Doing this could destroy the Complex."

She shook her head. Doing this would save the Complex. "I had hoped to reopen the mines once I had adequate control of the Rohen. That isn't possible."

"She told you that."

"I know what they are," Hendra snapped, standing from the table, and the man actually flinched. She smiled and stood straighter. "I have seen far more than any of you here."

"Have you?" Calder asked, his confident manner making her pause for a moment.

"I have," she returned, "and the Rohen must be destroyed."

"It can't be," Calder said.

"It can be disrupted. We saw that with the containment."

"And they worked out a way around that," Michaels interrupted. She glared at the little man across the table. Calder rested his hand on the man's shoulder, and he nodded once. Were they working on this against her? Had the Rohen or the hummer turned her greatest allies into a threat? She stepped back from the table. "General?" she asked, hoping someone would follow her instructions.

"I don't know," he admitted. "I haven't seen it, other than the fumes and the garden, which is gone, I understand."

"Moved," Michaels whispered, a faraway look in his eye. He sighed.

"Maybe it will move back," Calder offered, his voice soft and friendly. What had happened to this man?

"You think so?" Michaels asked, looking up at the man at his shoulder.

"Not if we blow it up," Calder added.

"Enough," Hendra bellowed. "This is not a debate; this is not up for a vote. I am the only vote and the only one to direct where this goes. The mines are to be destroyed. Start with Urgway."

"Which ones?" Calder asked.

"All of them."

He bowed his head, but no one moved. No one seemed to be taking any of the action she required from them.

"What of the chief?" the general asked.

"What of him?"

"He may not like your actions on his planet."

"It is my planet first. It is my solar system—my Complex. And if they are all destroyed at the same time, then he won't have the chance to question any of it."

"That would be a big job, and we can't be sure that destroying the mines will destroy the Rohen."

"It will go some way and prevent it being used by the people. What did you learn in your experiments about what could kill it?"

"It is a metal," Michaels murmured as though she had no idea what she was talking about.

"She could hear it screaming," Calder murmured.

"It didn't like being contained," Michaels went on. "You knew that much. I think it was willing to be tested, as it were. But not being able to leave as it wanted is what caused the distress. I don't know that anything could destroy it."

"I wouldn't be so sure," Hendra muttered. "Try. You can set a starduster to disintegrate a man; surely we have the weapons to do the same to metal."

"It isn't just any metal," Michaels whined.

"Set it up!" she snapped.

Michaels pushed his chair back, bowed and left the room, the general not far behind. But Calder remained, standing by the table and watching her. It wasn't with his usual concern.

"You have your orders."

He continued to stare.

"What happened to you while you were running around with the hummer?"

"The Rohen, or whatever it truly is, is somewhat determined."

"Which is why it must go."

He shook his head as though she wasn't listening and headed for the door. Again, it was the main door of the office, and she wondered what he was doing with his time. "Where are you going?"

"Didn't you task me with something?"

She nodded mutely.

He bowed his head and left.

Calder moved slowly through the building, making his way towards the pit, the large open space where the ships of the Hendra sat out together. It wasn't that he was taking the most direct route, but it was the most visible. And it wasn't that he held any fear of the dark passages he usually used, or what might be lurking in the smaller confined spaces, but there was a nervousness he didn't quite understand after the building had collapsed around him and left him standing in an open forest. It had been as though it was the first time he could breathe.

And despite promising to do as Hendra had asked, he had just as many concerns as Michaels did. More so, because he knew Isla's words spoken in anger rang true—that it was his fault this had happened. It was his willingness to follow Hendra's order into the cavern that day, into the unknown against an enemy he didn't understand and one he'd believed she did.

And then she had lied to him, given him what he had asked for but only after he had led his unit in to be slaughtered. The image of a frightened Isla, standing in the middle of the fighting, holding a duster she couldn't use, replayed in his mind. But they hadn't meant to harm her. They had worked around her, and yet he had been expendable. They all were. He understood what a soldier was, but despite all that had occurred with Hendra and what had followed, she was still willing to sacrifice him.

Surely as the head of the Rohendra Complex, she had to work for the benefit of the whole Complex. He had thought that was what she was doing. But it wasn't making the sense that it had. His doubt in her was growing, and it had started long before he had seen his own face among the dead. Not his face, he reminded himself with a shake of his head. Kalli's face—and he had let him go long ago.

At least he thought he had. And yet a girl and her Rohen copy kept calling him by that name, and it was starting to stir in him something he had thought long gone. Something he needed to be long gone. Kalli might have been friendly and smiley, but he hadn't been willing to sacrifice for the Complex—not completely. He'd had to die to allow Calder to do as he must, and yet Calder wondered now if he was doing the right thing. Maybe Kalli had a better understanding of the world. He stomped across the open space, barely glaring at those around him, but there was a general buzz in the air and men were moving quickly and methodically.

There was a time not so long ago when he would have coordinated such an event. But the general would have it in hand, and he seemed to be more willing than Calder to follow blindly along with what Hendra wanted from them. He hadn't even noticed any orders coming his way. But he knew what he was expected to do, even if he wasn't willing to do it himself.

There was nothing at the mines, he was sure. The Rohen could disappear, could run away through the porous sands of Urgway. There were mines on other planets, although he didn't think they were the same. Actually, he couldn't remember visiting any of them. He wondered if Isla had a better idea of what might have been going on around the Complex, despite her hiding on Urgway for so long.

Had she truly been hiding? He ran his hands over the controls of his ship, unaware of when he had climbed aboard, and made his way out into the sky ahead of the carriers vying for approval to leave first. But he didn't know where he should go. Was it to Draroh to find her and a way to make this right? But then, what was right? Maybe the Hendra had a point and the destruction of the mines would be enough. Although how filling in holes in the ground would do that, he couldn't understand. And if the Rohen then openly attacked the people... she would be justified in her approach.

He hung his head, running his fingers through his short hair. He had no idea where he was going or what he was doing, and it was a new feeling. He had been feeling somewhat lost since he had arrived on Draroh, which had intensified just before he'd returned to Rennet. He understood that Hendra was not what he'd thought she was, or at least she didn't consider him to be the ally he had tried to be for so long.

Isla kept returning to his mind, and Gray. He sighed. The boy had been something once, but he couldn't understand her attraction to him. Not that they had formed some strange team—that had happened long ago—but something else had happened since, something more than a friendship, a deep connection. He wondered if it was because Gray had some way with the strange words and she could hum.

Kalli would never have been enough for her. He would never have allowed himself the time to understand just who Island Tarle was, and now that he wanted to, someone else had beaten him to it.

He sucked in a deep breath and landed on the outskirts of the city. She had worked with him, confident he would help her even though he hadn't been so sure of that himself. He had to find a way—had to prove he was still Calder, for that was who he had chosen to be. He straightened his back and lifted from the ground. As he broke through the atmosphere, he brushed his hand over the comms panel.

"General," he said, trying to sound as calm as he wanted to be.

"Rick?"

"What do you need me to do?"

"Are you following the transports to Urgway?"

He nodded once and then remembered the general couldn't see him. "Yes sir."

There was a pause at the other end of the line. "Go to the main mine," the general directed. "You can coordinate from there. I am with the mining managers now."

"Yes sir."

The line disconnected, and he felt more confident than he had in days.

Sixteen

Isla studied the wall of Rohen rippling before her as Gray's hand slipped into hers. Firm and warm, and he was calm.

"You've done this before," she said.

He nodded and smiled. She realised he was smiling far more than he had previously. She only hoped their new connection helped rather than hindered what was to come.

"Will this take us to where we need to go?"

"Exactly," the minister said, his soft voice behind them, but Isla kept her eyes on the wall.

"Does it know, or do I need to know where I'm going?"

"You do know where you are going," Gray whispered.

"Do I?"

He gave a small laugh and stepped towards the wall. Isla gripped tighter to his hold and felt a wave of guilt that she was taking one man to save another. But it was what she had to do, no matter that she didn't understand how or why the Rohen would want her to help him. Particularly when she struggled to see Kalli in the man who had dragged her around the facilities, trying to help her find answers. His helping her had been far more about helping Hendra.

Kalli was gone—she had seen it in the books Gray had read to her. Kalli was long gone.

She blinked as the cold covered her skin, and then it was warm and comfortable and familiar as she stood in a cavern she knew far beneath the surface. The gentle glow of the trees and the fungi surrounding her lit up the world.

Gray smiled again, his hand still in hers and his brow creasing a little as he looked around. "Why here?"

"I was thinking of Kalli."

"Does he know these forests exist?"

She wanted to say no, but then the fight with the Rohen had been somewhere like this, where she had nearly died and it appeared he had. An underground forest, but it had been silver. Hadn't it? Or was that just the appearance as portrayed by Gray, in the blues and silver images that leapt to life at the sound of his voice?

"Was it in the trees, or the silver garden?"

"The fight?" he asked, understanding what she was asking. She was reminded that they had worked well as a team long before she'd been working with Calder. She nodded. He closed his eyes as though remembering the story he had read aloud, his lips moving silently in a language she would never understand.

"Trees," he murmured, then looked around at the space and back at her. "Not here."

"But a forest beneath the ground?" she asked.

"He therefore knows about these caverns."

"Maybe. Maybe he thought it a one-off."

"Could they find them again?"

"Would they want to?"

"She will be planning something now. The containment didn't work; the Complex is in uproar, the facilities abandoned. What would she do?"

"I don't know," Gray admitted, looking back at the trees. "But if you were thinking of him and we came here, then Calder is nearby."

Isla looked around, half expecting him to step out into the cavern. Would the Rohen allow him into the space again after what had occurred before? The forests were important on all the planets, and she wondered just what the Hendra might do to stop the Rohen. Might she damage the plants, destroy the trees? That had been the fear before. It had come to her after she had seen the fight play out that last time, the clear memories of her fear for the trees. Not for herself—she had known the damage to the trees would be more than the Complex could return from.

"She is going to destroy it all," Isla whispered.

"What?"

"Hendra will try to destroy the forests, and that in turn will destroy the Complex. It won't survive such an attack."

"Everywhere?"

"Maybe here first, where it can't be seen, and then she would take her attack to the other planets. We need to get to the surface and find Calder."

Gray shook his head, but he had been happy enough to follow her. She closed her eyes and stepped forward, taking Gray with her. They stood in a dark tunnel, watching soldiers creep ahead of them. None of whom were Calder. Her guess had been correct that they were laying charges, and the mine was going to be destroyed.

She put her hand over the nearest charge, and the mechanism stopped. It might have been designed to destroy the Rohen, but the universe was made of it. Just as she had removed a duster from Calder, she pulled the Rohen from the explosive and it vanished to nothing.

"This will be easy. You just run around the mine and destroy the charges."

"And if there isn't enough time? If there are other charges I can't find, or in other mines?" She stopped. Just as when she'd realised there were more facilities out there, more hummers in captivity, she knew there were many mines across this planet, and she was sure there were more soldiers in each.

"We have to go up," she said.

"Up? The surface?"

"He can stop this." She knew with every part of her. But whether he would, was another matter entirely.

She was walking through the building she had been in once before with strange offices and no tech.

"How did you...?" a soldier stammered as she appeared in a room, Gray a step behind.

"Colonel Calder?" she said.

"Do I look like—?"

"Where is he?" she asked, her voice firm. The room shook with the vibration, and for a moment she thought she was too late and the explosives had detonated. If they went off around the planet, there might not be an Urgway left to clean up. "Now!" she demanded.

"Here," Calder said, appearing in the doorway. "You know how to make an entrance." His cool blue eyes focused on her alone. He waved the other man towards the door and, although he protested, he did as directed. Calder ensured the door was closed behind him.

"You know what is planned," she said.

He nodded once.

"You understand what that will do," she continued, "yet you are still helping."

"I'm not sure what I am after spending time with you." His voice was not as sharp, something almost sad as he looked at Gray over her shoulder.

"Why here?" she asked.

"The mines are integral to the people accessing the Rohen. If that can be stopped, Hendra feels it will disrupt the Rohen enough that she will win."

"She can't win," Isla said.

"She will win—she is Hendra."

"That doesn't make it right," Gray whispered.

"But it is the way of the world. The Hendra has been in control for longer than any of the history books tell us," Calder insisted. "We can't change that."

"We can try," Gray went on. "And I don't think they have ruled independently. Something changed when her father died. Something changed in the way she understood the Rohen. The Hendra has always worked with the Rohen, and now she doesn't want to share."

Calder sighed and looked down at the ground. Isla was sure there were other selfish Hendras in the past who might have questioned whether they wanted to do this together. And yet they had, for the good of the Complex, and the people had never known of the partnership. This Hendra was going to destroy it all in a day and take the Complex down with her.

"It needs to stop. You have seen the trees."

"The trees?" he asked, confusion creasing his brow. He shook his head.

"The fight in the trees—she knew where the Rohen could be found. You found the trees."

Calder shook his head again. Could he not remember what he'd learnt as Kalli? "You don't remember what it was to be Kalli," she said kindly.

"I am not him anymore. It doesn't matter. I wasn't here," he said, something almost desperate in the way he spoke. As though he wanted to believe what he told her, and yet he didn't.

Isla stepped forward and grabbed the front of his suit, and without hesitation they were back in the cavern with the forest. "You have been here before," she said, trying to press upon him what the world was.

He looked around, stepping away from her, and she released Gray's hand. Had she taken it, or had he known what she would do and taken hers first?

Calder shuddered and looked around the trees. It was like any other forest, but as he looked up beyond the treetops, he was too aware that they were underground. "How?" he murmured.

"This is like the place you sent us into," Isla said, holding something back as though she wanted to remind him that he had been there but wasn't going to. "You knew it was underground."

He nodded, but he didn't remember the extent of what he hadn't known. He'd known what he was sending them to, but not where. "I must have known something. It was only the two of us."

"She lied to you," Isla said softly, as though she understood his hurt.

But he didn't get hurt; that wasn't what he was. He was a soldier who did as was needed for the good of the Complex. That was why he had worked so well with Hendra, why she had selected him to work directly with her. He had gained some other benefits of the position, although that had been influenced by more than just her power. He had admired her, what she stood for and how she acted. As he looked at the woman standing before him now, he realised he hadn't really thought about what he was doing or what he should have been focused on. Hendra was only interested in herself and her own needs. Isla was determined to save them all, and he had nearly prevented that.

"She thought she was doing as she had to."

"You know the truth, and yet you still defend her," Gray murmured behind Isla.

"It is what I need to do," Calder said. *Gray didn't understand what he was. Who he was.* "It is what I am."

Isla raised her hand as though to placate him, and Gray nodded slowly. Maybe he understood more than Calder had given him credit for.

"Was it here?" Isla asked.

Calder shook his head. Although he wasn't sure, he knew he hadn't been in this forest before. He knew this was somewhere different. "How many of these forests exist?"

"Many," she whispered.

Something worried Calder, something to do with the trees. The fear he had seen in Isla that day seemed to make sense. "They are connected," he said. Although how he knew that, he wasn't sure.

She nodded.

He pressed the communicator at his neck. "General, we have a problem."

"What kind of problem?" came the static reply.

"There is more living within the mines than what the Hendra wishes to destroy."

He couldn't hear the response. It might have been a curse; it might have been something else that was lost to the static and rock between them.

"Sir, I'm underground."

The curse was clear and loud that time.

"When is the attack to occur?" Isla asked.

He shrugged. The preparations would take some time, but when they were to actually detonate the explosives was an unknown. At least to him.

"Get your arse up here, Colonel!" came the stern voice of the general as though he were standing beside him, and Calder was startled by the clarity of the voice.

"I'm not quite sure how to do that. I might have taken a wrong turn," he lied too easily. He had done it most of his career. Although he had never lied to Hendra, he wondered if she would notice if he did.

He also wasn't sure if it was enough—if the threat, unsaid as it was, would stop the attack. Would Hendra blow him up anyway?

⚫

Gray tried to maintain his calm, but it was hard. Did he look as though he was helping, or was Calder giving away the secrets of the mines? The secrets of the Rohen?

"I don't know if that is enough," Calder said. He sounded almost apologetic, and Isla gave him a small nod. Did she really know what they could do to stop this?

Gray took another steadying breath and then looked up at the two of them watching him too closely. Isla gave him a warm smile. Only a step away, she reached for his hand and gave it a gentle squeeze.

"You don't trust him," she whispered, despite the other man being only just a few steps away. Calder looked away to the trees then, annoyed.

"I trust you," Gray said. "Will he help, or will he just try to find another way to do as Hendra wants?"

"I don't think Hendra is doing this for the right reasons," Calder murmured.

The admission took Gray by surprise. He pressed his lips closed in the hope he wouldn't say anything to anger him. Or make him change his mind.

"Why do you say that?" Isla asked. "What did you see?"

"What you wanted me to," Calder snapped. The anger only flashed across his face before it was replaced with something else, something Gray couldn't read. He looked lost.

"I wanted to know the truth," Isla said as a small shudder crossed her skin, and Gray closed his hand tighter around hers. He had hoped that her seeing the truth would help. He remembered the words, but it didn't play out the same way unless he was reading. Or was it only a single word?

He released her hand and stepped closer to the trees. What was the word for where they were, and was it similar or the same for all the underground forests?

"Gray?" she asked softly behind him, but he shook his head, trying to find the word he knew was there. And then it was, as though given to him by the trees he studied, and when he said it aloud, they glowed that bit brighter.

"What did you do?" Calder asked. It wasn't accusatory—it was with wonder.

"That is where we are," Gray said, looking over the trees and knowing it was this place only.

"Do you know where we were?" Isla asked.

He did. He understood the name, the place that called.

"Tell me," she whispered, so close and yet she wasn't holding him.

He said the name as it formed clearly in his mind.

"Again," Isla said, her hand in his, and then they were there. In a forest beneath the surface of the planet, the one he had seen in his readings, the one he had played out for her. He half expected to see the bodies still strewn across the forest floor.

Isla let go of his hand and walked to the nearest tree. Stretching out her hand, she leaned into it. She smiled as she rested her forehead against the bark.

Calder caught Gray's attention as he put his hand to his throat. "Repeat," he said.

"What are you doing?" Gray asked, wondering if he was calling people to this cavern, but he was unsure they could truly find it again.

"Someone is trying to reach me. All I'm getting is static."

"Leave him," Isla whispered.

"They might turn the mines over to find him," Gray said.

"They may not," Calder returned, dropping his hand by his side.

Isla stepped away from the tree and turned to look over the clearing. Gray wished he could read what she was thinking, what she was trying to do. She looked up and gave him a warm smile. "I'm ok," she said.

He nodded once. Would he ever stop worrying about her?

"Say the name," Calder said, looking into the trees.

Gray allowed the word to fill his mind and whispered it into the trees. Like in the other cavern, they glowed, only it was brighter this time and the walls surrounding them were closer. He turned, taking in the space. There were no pathways here. No way for anyone to reach them.

"It is hidden," Isla said as though reading what he was thinking.

"Or we are trapped," Calder said.

"How do you think we got here?" Gray murmured.

The man turned and looked at him seriously, and Gray was somewhat relieved that the constant anger and desire to kill him had disappeared from his features.

"Why are you so angry all the time?" Gray asked. "Were you disappointed with what you became?"

Rather than answer, Calder sighed and looked away, walking towards the wall of the cavern.

"There is so much to take in," Isla whispered. "Allow him some time." She took his hand and pulled him into the trees. They still glowed. He ran his hand over the bark, taking in the texture, understanding something more of them than he had before. His time on Draroh had given him more than he'd expected.

For the first time, Gray wondered what that would mean for his future. If it was another divide between them despite the Rohen pulling them in the same direction. They were doing this to help—they had always been trying to help—and yet he understood the need to fear them. The concern as to when they might no longer need them and thus push them away or allow them to be taken by those they had been trying to stop.

Alone in the trees, he whispered the name of the place again, and Isla drew in a surprised breath as the world glowed gently around them. She ran her hand over a tree, then looked at her fingers as though the glow might have rubbed off onto her skin.

He wanted to see her skin in the light of the trees, but he silently allowed her to pull him further away from Calder and into the dense forest.

"What are you looking for?" he asked.

"A reason we were here," she responded without turning back to him. When he stopped, she continued to tug on his arm.

"The answer is not here."

Isla looked back at him with some amount of wariness. "How do you know?"

He shrugged. "I just do."

She stepped forward and ran a hand over the side of his face, her fingers barely touching his skin. "What did you become?"

"Nothing," he murmured. But hadn't he just been wondering the same thing—what he might be and what that might mean going forward?

"Calder," she called, and he tried not to groan as the other man loudly made his way between the trees towards them. When he appeared, she looked between the two of them. "Put your hand on that tree," she directed, and Calder did just that. When he opened his mouth to possibly ask why, Isla held up her finger. "Say the name," she directed Gray, who also did as he was told.

The trees glowed a little brighter again.

"What is it?" he asked.

She shook her head, studying Calder.

"Isla?" Calder asked, carefully removing his hand from the tree as the pale glow subsided.

"On Oric, the Rohen moved away from you, hid from you. I thought there was something it feared. Perhaps they did. But there isn't any of that here."

"You did say that the Rohen said he would help," Gray said.

"That was before Oric, and the reason I went with him. But..." She shook her head as though she couldn't make sense of it.

"Are we near a mine?" Calder asked.

"Do you want to report us?" Gray replied, and Calder gave him a flat look.

"If we are here when the charges are detonated, it might not matter what they think of any of us."

"She wouldn't blow you up."

"I wouldn't be so sure," Calder replied. But there was something certain in the way he spoke. "And right now, I can't make contact with anyone to tell them where we are—or that it isn't safe to blow the mines."

"Which are they blowing first?" Isla asked. "If we could be there, then we might have a chance..." She drifted off as Calder shook his head. "They will blow them all together."

"Yes, and that will not only destroy all of this, it will possibly weaken the structure of the planet. She hasn't thought this through."

"I think she has," Isla said. "I think she is very sure of what she is doing—she just hasn't considered what else it will do."

"She is going to destroy the Complex, one planet at a time," Gray whispered, hoping he was wrong. He thought it had meant something else when Isla had said it could be destroyed, but now he understood that she'd meant it in the literal sense.

"It won't matter if I am there or not. It won't stop her. She is too certain that the Rohen has to be stopped."

Calder pushed his way back out through the trees and, before Gray could give his opinion, Isla was following him.

"Are you sure she wouldn't want to keep you safe? You appear very close," Gray said.

Calder stopped, and Gray was already stepping back when he turned slowly. He didn't have the expression Gray expected, but rather one of someone who had lost something very dear to them. His career might have been that something, but Gray suspected there was far more to their relationship than anyone else could guess at. He might have actually cared about the woman.

"Why are you so sure?" Gray asked again, but his words were kinder.

"She lied to me," Calder said, walking towards the wall. "Are we able to get out or into the mine, or was there another way?"

Gray looked at Isla. She was the one who had brought them here. She was the one to take them back out again, but it would depend on where to. Did they need to be in a mine? Did they need to be in an office somewhere ensuring that the Hendra didn't give the order to detonate? They didn't need Calder to tell them anything. Between the two of them, they knew the Hendra and the Rohen best.

Gray had to admit that he had somewhat of a better understanding of the history of the Rohen now, and of what they needed. But he wasn't sure he was as clear on that message as others. The minister came to mind, bent over his desk, scratching away with his wooden pen across the parchment. Gray closed his eyes, remembering the long hours together as the minister wrote while he read. Absorbing everything he could and sharing some of it aloud with others, including Beth and Isla and Calder.

He had no idea if the words the minister wrote were those he then read, or if there was something else that occurred with his writing. He focused on Calder then, running his hands over the rough walls of the cavern and wondering if he thought he could really find a way out. "But you've been here before," he whispered.

Calder shook his head, but something in his stance had shifted. He wasn't the embodiment of rigid strength he always appeared to be; he was sagging, his shoulders hunched.

"Isla kept telling me I'd been there," he said, still facing the wall. "She was certain, and I would have been. I wouldn't have sent my unit into a fight like that and not been there, leading the way. Just as the recording said it was. I didn't know," he said, turning to take them in.

"That it would be the slaughter it was?" Gray asked.

"Nor that I was amongst the dead. She told me..." He took a deep breath. "She told me it was the perfect time to disappear, become the soldier she needed me to be."

"You don't remember?" Isla asked, her voice soft as she stepped towards Calder.

He shook his head, his distress becoming apparent. "Can you help me?"

"We can try," Gray said. "But it might be that you need to trust in others."

"You mean the Rohen," he said, his head bowed.

Isla nodded, and Gray was sure he caught a glimpse of silver from the corner of his eye.

Seventeen

C alder backed up slowly against the solid cavern wall as the Rohen's silvery form moved forward fluidly. It amazed Isla how humanoid they appeared—and yet so different at the same time.

She bowed her head and the Rohen stopped, taking her in and then looking towards Calder again. "Why are you here?" he asked, the deep timbre of his voice echoing from the walls.

"You know why," she said. "You understand what is happening."

"I am not sure that you can stop it."

"Excuse me?" Gray asked as though that was the last thing he expected the Rohen to say. "She is Island Tarle."

The silver form laughed. Although the sound carried through the space, the face didn't appear to move at all.

"Not quite all you thought she was," Calder quipped.

"Neither are you, Kalli," the form continued.

His face fell, and he pushed against the wall again.

"Have you remembered?" it asked.

Calder shook his head, as though shaking the idea away.

"But you know the truth of it."

"It might not be enough," Isla said. "He has been lied to for too long."

"Only by himself," the Rohen continued.

"We can stop this," Isla said. "We have to."

"That much is true, but whether you can stop someone so determined is another matter."

"You've seen it," Gray whispered.

The being turned to him and bowed, the movement making him appear uncomfortable. "I know what you are. You know what we are," it continued. "You will do as you see fit." Then it turned and walked back towards the trees.

"Will you let us out?" Calder called after it.

"You already are," came the whisper through the trees, although Isla could no longer see the Rohen.

"Do they always speak in riddles?" Calder snapped.

"I can take us to anywhere we need to be," Isla said. Only she had no idea where that should be. Could they convince those who were to destroy the planet to stop? She didn't want to leave anyone behind, and she didn't want to be blown up. Her task had been to save Kalli, and so far she seemed to have only broken him.

"What do you think we should do?" she asked him. "Where should we go?"

"Who is in charge of this event?" Gray asked, and although Isla knew that the Hendra was behind it, there would be someone else coordinating it. It might have been Calder, but it appeared he didn't hold the same trust as before.

"The general," Calder said, something in the way he said it making Isla wonder if he was disappointed by the outcome.

"So, we take this to the general," she said softly.

"I don't know," he murmured. "I can't see how it would help. My being underground was a delay, but one that won't last long. Most of the charges are already laid. As soon as I appear before him, he could detonate the lot."

Isla nodded slowly. She had no idea where they could go next, although she did understand very well that they couldn't allow the attack to take place. And there was no way she could remove the charges. Could the Rohen? She looked around then. Of course, it was something they could prevent or stop occurring. But it had to come from Hendra—she had to see the error of her ways.

Isla opened her mouth to ask how they could do such a thing when Calder held up his hand, the other at his throat. "Repeat," he murmured.

"I'll get you closer," Isla offered, holding out her hand to him as Gray slipped his hand in the other.

"There was something about a problem."

"What kind of problem?" Gray asked as they reappeared in the mine they had first entered.

"Not sure..." His hand was at his throat again. "It keeps breaking up."

An explosion overhead made them all crouch down, although what that would do, Isla didn't know. Either way, there was the chance of being trapped beneath the rock in the dark. She shuddered at the idea. The ground rumbled and dust fell from the roof of the tunnel, but nothing collapsed. The planet didn't appear to be breaking up around her.

"I want out of this," Gray muttered, and she realised he had been buried the last time they'd been in a situation like this.

"Up?" she asked, looking at Calder. He nodded, and they were walking into the building at the entrance to the mine.

"Colonel Calder?" someone asked as he strode ahead of them. "The General needs..." Another explosion rocked the building, and Gray grabbed at Isla's arm.

"Don't be afraid," she whispered.

He shook his head as though that wasn't it. Calder stopped and looked about.

"They are causing some issues," the soldier said.

"Who are?" Calder asked.

"Rebels. The general thought he could blame the whole event on them, but the explosions aren't anywhere near the mines. There are groups in the nearest cities claiming they are trying to protect the mining, that it should be restarted. That they will remove the Elite forces from the planet and save us all."

"And the people believe that?" Calder asked, sounding disbelieving and very much like he had before.

Isla wondered if the show was for the soldier or if it had been for her. Down in the mines and the forests, he had been a different man. Maybe he didn't want Hendra to understand what he had learnt. That he had been there, that she had lied to him and that he would work against her.

"Who is he helping here?" Gray whispered in her ear. He must have had the same thought.

"Us, I hope," she returned as quietly as she could.

"Where is the general?" Calder asked the soldier.

"This way, sir."

"So if the rebels are in the cities, what are they blowing up?" Gray asked.

"Elite ships, mostly. A couple of buildings went up earlier. I'm surprised you didn't feel it, sir."

"If they want the mines to reopen, why damage buildings?"

"I think they are trying to drive people, soldiers, out of the area. Once the Elite are gone, there would be nothing to stop them."

"Are there that many Elite here?" Calder asked.

Isla didn't think there were enough to man every mine on the planet, if that was the Hendra's aim.

"Enough to be noticed," the soldier said. Isla recognised his uniform as Hendra, but he wasn't Elite.

"They aren't targeting your ships?"

"Maybe they think we will side with them," he said, a little shyly.

"You may not be Elite," Isla said, "but you are still Hendra's men."

He stopped and saluted her. "Yes, ma'am, we are."

"Time you started acting like it," Calder murmured as he pushed past the young man and along a corridor. Stopping before a door like any other, he pressed his hand to the panel to open it. "General," he greeted the man behind the desk. Although he didn't salute him.

"You made it out then?" the general asked, barely looking up from the monitor before him.

Isla wondered where it had come from. The last few times she had been in this building, it had been surprisingly tech free. She doubted anything was left that could indicate the Elite was involved in anything to do with the mines. The general continued to watch whatever report or image was unfolding on the screen before him, and Calder glanced back at Isla before clearing his throat.

"I'm aware, Colonel."

"Are you?" Calder asked. "I'm somewhat out of the loop."

The older man looked up in surprise, and Isla wondered what he was surprised by—the fact that Calder was out of the loop, or that he would so openly say so? "I told you…" He drifted off, refocusing on the screen.

"The reception was patchy."

The general nodded but didn't look back up, and in the end Calder moved around the desk to stand behind him and look at the monitor himself.

"Who is that?" he asked.

"New advisor."

Calder's face grew hard, and he crossed his arms.

"Advisor to whom?" Gray asked,

"The Hendra has some concerns with…" He looked up again, taking in Gray and then looking at Isla. He turned back to Calder with a look that asked what he was up to.

"What is she doing?" Calder asked.

"Finding a way to try and end her problem."

"She is only making more issues for the whole Complex if she tries to continue with this."

"You said that before," the general said, looking back to the monitor.

"We don't know that these explosions won't do more than just collapse the mines. I got lost down there." Calder sounded so sincere. "Those tunnels run for miles in all directions. An explosion might end up deeper than we thought and lead out under the cities."

"Hmmm," was all the general said, still preoccupied with the monitor.

"Who is that?" Calder asked, clearly frustrated that he didn't know the person. Isla was tempted to step around the desk as well.

"Some scientist."

"Where is Michaels?"

"Unfortunately, he was starting to sound like you—and she wasn't happy with that. He's off exploring some new avenue."

"She sent him off, or he went willingly?"

Gray made a strange noise, and Isla looked towards him.

"Not the garden," the general said as though he understood what they might be worried about. But then, they were on Urgway, with the Hendra keen to blow the whole planet away. She didn't care if the garden survived; in fact, she was likely hoping it didn't. The more she could destroy of the Rohen, the better her world, the safer her universe. Only she was so wrong.

"When is the detonation?" Calder asked.

The general shook his head and waved his hand dismissively.

"I'd rather not be this close when it happens," Calder continued.

"It won't be happening. Not with the rebels."

"Tell me about them," Calder prompted. Isla had been keen to ask the question herself, but she didn't think the general would share anything with her.

"Nothing much to tell other than they are causing more of a headache than you at the moment. We hoped we could turn it around, make it appear that they were responsible, but they are staying clear of any mines. The chain reaction we were hoping to make appear to happen is likely to do just what you claim," the general said, sounding disappointed. "But we need to find a way around that—achieve what she wants while making it look as though she had nothing to do with any of it."

"How does the chief feel about this happening on his planet?" Isla asked.

"It isn't his," Calder said, his eyes on the monitor.

All eyes turned to him. Even the general looked up.

"The Hendra sees the entire Complex as hers. And that is the reason she won't share it with the Rohen."

"It isn't hers to share," Gray said, his voice low. It sounded as though he knew something the others didn't.

Isla thought it a partnership. The stories or histories he had read to her certainly appeared to be something like that, but she wasn't privy to much of what was in that library. It might be that there was far more to the relationship and their understanding of the universe and the Complex than the Hendra could ever have.

"What was she told?" Isla asked.

"When?" Calder asked.

"Growing up, learning to be what she is. What was she told about the Rohen and the Complex?"

He shook his head. "I have no idea."

"She hasn't talked about it? What about before the last attack?"

"What attack?" the general asked.

Calder glared and shook his head, but Isla knew someone had to know what had happened. Someone had to know why the Hendra was so determined to destroy what she wanted to control.

"The one I survived."

"It wasn't clear what happened," the general said, looking up at Calder again. "Or where you were, or what you faced."

"I was there," she whispered.

"I lived through the recordings, just as you did. I might not have been there, but I relived every moment. What makes you think the Rohen was involved?"

"I was there," she said again. "The recordings were doctored. The battleground never disclosed."

"No," he said clearly as he stood, and the monitor blinked out. "You don't remember clearly."

"I remember it better now than the story I was told of what happened. I've seen it. I've revisited the ground where it happened."

"I half expected to see the blood still on the ground," Calder whispered. Gray opened his mouth and then closed it.

"You weren't even there," the general snapped. "You were to bring her into the fold, and now you are following her stories as though they were your own. Are you trying to tell me the attack you survived was here on Urgway?"

"Yes," Calder said before Isla could answer. "I was there."

The general looked at him as though seeing him for the first time.

"You know," Calder accused. It might be that Hendra had been keeping more secrets than Calder had originally thought.

"If you were there, then I could guess."

"This can't happen," Gray interrupted. "These attacks on the mines will destroy more than the planet."

"What will you do now?" Isla asked.

"Rebels," the general muttered, "are everywhere. As though they knew we were coming—as though they knew what we were trying to do."

Isla felt the weight lift somewhat from her shoulders. "Perhaps they do," she said.

Hendra studied the two men sitting across from her at the table in her office. Why hadn't she been warned they were coming? There was a lot she had to do, and now she had rebels making her life hard.

Minister Burre she knew only by name and reputation. Despite his being her father-in-law, she had never spent any time with him other than at the wedding. Alice had always said he was busy, that he had important work to do for the Chief of Draroh—or was it with the chief? She wasn't sure and, looking at them now, she wasn't sure she trusted either of them.

"I had hoped to see Alice while I was here," the minister said.

Hendra gulped down the rising fear and tears welling inside her. She couldn't tell this man the truth about his daughter because she didn't know what that was. She had thought Alice dead, although Island Tarle was sure she was alive and Calder had backed that theory up. But her trust in him was slipping, and she wasn't sure she was ready to deal with that either. Something had happened while they'd been away, and she had no idea what it was or how to respond.

"She's not here at the moment."

"Oh," he said, "that is disappointing. I'm sure she has much to do."

The Hendra bent her head in acknowledgement and wondered if he could possibly know anything of where Alice might be or what she had been planning.

"I wanted to offer my congratulations on your impending mother-hood," he said, his smile wide and apparently genuine.

"I'm sure you will get the chance to see her before you leave. How long do you plan for your visit to last?" she asked the chief of Draroh.

"Whatever it takes," he said. "We have not fixed plans."

The minister smiled at her again, and she wondered why he had come all this way when he had never made the effort before. As an advisor to the chief, she wouldn't expect he would be busy enough on Draroh.

"I see you have a new advisor," the minister said, still smiling, as though he had read her mind.

"I like to take as much advice as I can, from as many areas of society as I can."

His smile broadened. "Can I offer you some advice?"

She bowed her head, wondering just what this man might suggest.

"That you focus on your child's future."

"Always," she said, trying to smile in return and not take offence at his words. As her father-in-law, he might have some interest in a grandchild.

"And stop what you are trying to do," he continued.

She glared at him.

"Calder stayed with you," she said.

"The colonel? Yes, he did on a recent visit to Draroh. I do not believe he understood our familial connection at the time."

"Alice talked little of home."

The chief smiled again, and she wondered what he thought of the idea—then silently cursed herself for using the past tense. Alice was already gone in her mind, whether that was dead or run away. She still couldn't understand why her wife would have acted against her, what might have led to it or influenced her.

"You want the child to survive," she whispered.

"Of course, I do. The children are the future of the Complex, and your child is the most special of them all."

She wasn't sure how to respond, and she couldn't make her face smile any longer.

"Alice was poisoning me," she said.

"I don't think that is right," the chief said. "Alice cares for you and your child."

Hendra shook her head.

"I think you might be confused," the minister added.

"I am not," she said, standing from the table and walking across the room to look out the window. The child had grown over the last short while; she felt the movement more often, and it was a wonder. She wanted to put her hand to her belly and feel the movement on the outside as well as the inside, but she remained still. Alice had said she would come to appreciate what it was to hold the growing child inside her, but she wouldn't give the satisfaction to anyone connected to Alice.

"Rohen," she said, trying to bring her thoughts back to the reason they were here. Which neither of them had yet to make clear.

The minister nodded once.

"She put Rohen in my food."

The chief looked at the minister but said nothing.

"You don't believe me," she said, walking back towards the table. "You know what she did, and you are hiding her."

The chief shook his head, but the minister cocked his head to the side.

"What are you doing?" he asked.

"It is not your place to question me," she said, her voice too loud, but she couldn't continue to deal with his smiling.

"The mines," the minister said as though she hadn't spoken.

"They are illegal, as per my orders, and I am looking at ways to permanently decommission them."

"Permanently? You understand that the people want them to remain open?"

"It doesn't matter what they want. The mines are not safe, and as Hendra it is my place to ensure the safety of the people."

"You aren't doing that. You are ensuring your own safety."

"I am not at risk," she said slowly, wondering if this was a threat. For a heartbeat, she wished Calder were here to watch over her, but he hadn't been himself lately. His stay with this man might well have been one of the reasons for that change.

"Your position is never at risk."

"But I might be?"

The minister smiled again, and she knew there was more to his words than she could make sense of.

"Chief, you are very quiet on this matter. Not that I sought an opinion, but your minister is keen to give it."

"There is nothing of value I can add to the conversation. And I doubt you would listen to me if I could."

Hendra sighed, and the child squirmed within her. "I am unsure as to why you came at all."

"I doubt your advisor," the minister said.

"You are to advise your chief, not me. And in all the years I have known your daughter, I am yet to understand what you are minister of."

"There are other ministers," the chief said as though it explained away any doubt.

"Are there?" she asked. It wasn't a role she had heard used by the other chiefs. And she didn't have one.

She looked at the man who had seemed so friendly at the wedding, so keen to give his daughter to the leader of the universe. Did he just want power? Did he see her as able to support him rather than the other way around?

"Child, you have no idea of the world," the minister said.

"I understand far more of it that you are even privy to," she said. Then she looked at him as though seeing him for the very first time. "Rohen," she breathed.

He stood then and bowed his head. "Your father understood, as did the Hendra before him. You are a selfish child. Do not destroy what you have been tasked to care for with your selfishness."

As he turned for the door, the chief stood, bowed his head and followed. She wondered then who led who. Did the minister have more power than the chief of Draroh?

"I'm not finished," she said.

He stopped at the door and turned back. "If you do not change your ways, you will be."

Hendra opened her mouth, and he turned away again. As the door closed behind them, she raced across the room. She didn't care who this man was to either her wife, the chief or herself—he would not threaten her.

She wrenched the door open to find the space beyond empty.

The secretary looked up from his desk, stood and bowed.

"Where did they go?" she demanded.

"Who?"

"The chief and the minister."

"Were they coming by? I didn't receive any notification."

"They just left!" she screamed at the idiot as he slowly shook his head. She stepped back and closed the door. The idea of Island Tarle appearing in her office made her sit down on the floor. She put her hands to her belly, cradling the child protected within her. How many others were working with the Rohen?

The rohen weren't working for the Complex, they were working for themselves. Her father had said as much, hadn't he, as he lay dying. He had talked so extensively of them, what they did, and what they would bring to the Complex. And then in those last moments there was something else, something like fear of what they were and she knew what she had to do.

Eighteen

Calder paced in the small office while Isla sat far too close to Gray. He wanted to wrench her away from him, although he wasn't sure why. Perhaps because she believed in him. He had thought he had that same trust from Hendra, but he didn't. And not only did he not trust Hendra, now he couldn't trust his own decision-making.

"I want to talk to them," Isla said.

He shook his head and kept pacing. It wouldn't do any good. She thought she could help in some way—that if the people understood, she could convince them she could save the Rohen and stop the Hendra. He was sure she would just be branded a heretic. She was already a wanted criminal, or at least she had been, and he knew the chief of Urgway had limited tolerance for her. She had nearly brought down his racing industry. Although Calder knew she wasn't the one responsible. He stopped and turned back to see her looking at him expectantly.

"You know I was behind the race," he said.

"I guessed."

"You know I tried to kill you."

"Several times," Gray said, reaching for her hand. Calder tried not to react to the movement.

"I'm not the one who could help you."

"And yet you are," she said.

"You know the world is not as it has been, and you know Hendra will destroy it," Gray said.

Calder grumbled, but they were right. "How do you know they will listen?"

"Because they care about the Complex too."

He shook his head, but headed for the door. When a message came through from Hendra, he stopped dead.

"I want you here."

"I'm busy," he murmured, and Isla stood slowly from the chair.

"I am under threat," Hendra whispered.

"You are the threat." Calder pulled at the patch at his throat and screwed it into a ball before dropping it onto the floor. "Fine," he murmured. "How you think you can get close to these people? I have no idea."

"Honestly," she replied, "neither do I."

"Can you guess at who is in control of this rebellion?" Gray asked, and by the tone of his voice it appeared he could.

"Where were you on this planet?" Calder asked.

Gray raised his hand and opened his mouth, then allowed the hand to drop and shook his head.

"He is to help us," Isla whispered.

"You are the only one to believe that," Gray whispered back to her.

Calder knew he was right. He wasn't even sure what he was doing, let alone who he was helping.

"Maybe those you knew could help us," she pressed.

"I don't think they are involved in this."

"How can you be sure?" Calder asked. "You've been gone some time. And do you really know who you were working with?"

"I wouldn't say I ever really worked with them."

"I saw..." Isla started, then looked to Calder.

"Reilly knew far more than I did."

Isla rested her hand on Gray's arm, and Calder rolled his shoulders. Was he going to be constantly reminded of every ill he had done this man? And what if they found the rebels he had been working with or Isla got the chance to talk to anyone? Who was to say they would listen, and what did he want them listening to? When he refocused, Gray was wiping at the corner of his eye and Isla was threading her arms around his waist.

"What good will it do?" Calder asked. "What can you really do to stop this? You can pull things from the air and move about unseen. Why are you even asking for my assistance in this or for me to go with you?" His voice was too loud for the small area, and he knew it. He was lost and wanted to know what side he was on, but he didn't know who to ask.

He shook his head as Isla took a step towards him, and she stopped. She glanced back at Gray.

"And you," Calder said, looking directly at the man for the first time in too long, "can read books."

"Who knew?" Gray quipped, and Calder sucked in a breath. "I'm also good with a duster."

"I have lost men to prove that," Calder muttered.

"Don't." Gray bristled. If he had hackles, Calder was sure they would be standing up. "You locked her away to experiment on," he said, putting his hand on Isla's shoulder. "You killed Reilly. You nearly managed to kill me. You are not what the Rohen keep trying to tell us you are."

"And what is that?" he asked.

"Kalli," Isla said softly.

Calder shook his head. He'd been right when he'd said Kalli was long gone. And he was. It didn't matter what Hendra had done or when she had done it. That had been the plan. That had been his wish—to be someone else, someone stronger. And he was. Kalli might have been the soldier he had wanted to be, the leader he had wanted to be, but he had never been strong enough to do what needed to be done.

"We'll go alone." Gray headed for the door.

"You won't get anywhere without me," Calder said.

Isla reached out and took Gray by the arm, and they were gone in a heartbeat.

Isla breathed out slowly in the dark cavern. The heat of the planet's surface blew inside, reminding her of her first time in this space as she felt the hum of the machinery around her. She had been so frustrated with Gray at the time that she didn't even want to know who he was or what he was up to.

She had known there was more to this place than a group of people hiding. And it was likely they were all connected to Calder in some way. Or maybe, if the Rohen were involved, they knew Kalli and that he needed saving.

She jumped as Gray touched her arm. "Are you afraid?"

"Not of the dark," she said. "Although I'm not sure what comes next, how I can help him and how I can stop the Hendra."

"She will need someone to blame," he said. "We want to be sure that someone isn't us."

"I don't think she is thinking that clearly. If she can't blame the rebels as she hoped, she might just blow the mines to prove she was right in claiming them dangerous."

"She will blame the Rohen itself," Gray said, standing in closer, and Isla nodded despite the dark.

Their fingers interlocked as they made their way along the tunnel towards the dim light at the end. She still wasn't sure what they would come across and who they would meet. Could these people really be working with the Rohen, unknowingly, to save a world they didn't realise was under such threat? Isla was sure these people just wanted to be out from under Hendra's rule, and possibly even the rule of the chief. But they might be the only option.

"Does Calder want to help?" Gray asked.

"I don't think he knows quite what he is."

"Wasn't that your task—to show him?"

She shrugged. She wasn't sure herself what she was or what she was meant to be doing. Saving Kalli had turned out to be much harder than she imagined. She had seen glimpses of him before, she thought, but she didn't know the man who had paced that small office with the doubt in his eyes.

Gray slowed her walk, tugging on her hand, yet he was moving in front of her as though to shield her from what might be inside the chamber. As they stepped into the light, she could only see ships. She remembered her own racer here at some point, and the boy who looked after it. The space was quiet now, only the slight hum of Rohen moving through the world around them indicating there was any life at all.

Their boots echoed on the hard floor as they wove their way between the ships and into an area she had tried so hard not to take in the last time. She hadn't wanted to appear as a threat. She hadn't cared then—she'd just wanted to get back to her racing. Which now seemed so long ago.

There was no one at the consoles, and no one in the medical room where Gray had been treated. The weapons she had thought they'd had were gone. She ran her hand over a panel at one of the consoles, but nothing appeared.

"Where are they?" Gray asked.

"I don't think they were ever here."

"Don't say that. Reilly was here. He worked with them. He knew them. You saw them."

She nodded, and she wondered if the Rohen had worked with Reilly for a reason. Was Gray that reason? He stood in the middle of the space, looking around as though it didn't make any sense.

"It would be in a book," she whispered.

He closed his eyes as though remembering what he had read. Then he shook his head once, his eyes still closed. She watched him for too long as he stood in silence. She didn't know what to do or where to go.

"You were given a mission," a deep voice flowed through her, and she turned to take in the shimmering Rohen behind her.

"I can't complete it. He doesn't exist."

"He does."

"He is gone," she said, feeling her frustration push out across the space. "Hendra would destroy it all. Shouldn't I be trying to find a way to prevent that?"

"You will, if you work on the task given."

"By helping Kalli, saving Kalli, I can stop the Hendra destroying the Complex? We can't even get her to listen to the man about what she will do if she tries to blow up the mines. Then she would move on to another planet. She is blinded by her fear."

"She is what she is," he said. "You are as you are. Save Kalli." The Rohen disappeared.

She rubbed at her eyes and looked up at Gray watching her. She tried to smile for him, but she couldn't find the energy. She didn't know how to do what they needed her to. He would never be what he had been. Kalli was gone. Calder, despite his uncertainty, would back Hendra.

"You don't think you can," Gray said softly, closing his arms around her.

"I think he has gone. He believes it. Who am I to find anything different?"

"He has lost trust. He just destroyed his connection with Hendra."

Isla shook her head against his chest. "They will always be connected. There will always be something that drags them back together."

"The child," he whispered over her hair.

"It is not his. He believed it was, yet I think Alice and the Rohen created that child. Hendra couldn't have children. Calder knew that—he was privy to more than he should have been—and yet she fell pregnant easily enough."

"What if the Rohen used him to create their queen?"

"How?"

"How do they do anything? What if they did something during the attack?"

"I don't know anymore," she said. "I don't know where to go or what to do, or how to stop any of this from happening."

"Save Kalli," whispered around the walls.

"I don't know how!" she screamed, pushing out of Gray's arms. When she saw the disappointment on his face, she stepped back up to him and rested her hands on his chest. "If we stop this on Urgway, can we stop whatever else comes next?"

"Maybe to save him, we have to take this to Hendra."

"Get her to tell him the truth?" Isla asked. "I'm not sure she would do that. And would it help?"

"It is all we have."

Nineteen

C **hapte**
Isla tried to sit still, but it was harder than she imagined it could be. Calder still paced back and forth, and Gray stood too close behind her. It was the woman before her that made her fidget. She had faced Hendra often enough now. Although the leader of the Complex thought she knew best, it was hard to make her see what needed to be done.

"You know what they are," Hendra finally said, and Calder's pacing paused.

Isla bowed her head, but she wasn't sure what she could say.

The Hendra looked at her for a moment. Something of recognition flashed across her face, but she returned to the stoic anger of earlier before Isla could understand what she thought she knew.

"What is it?" Calder asked, striding towards the table, and the Hendra leaned back from his approach. He must have seen it too and, knowing Hendra better than most, he knew what it meant.

"Nothing," Hendra said. "Only that she works with the enemy. She has been leading you away."

"Away from what?" he snapped, then ran his fingers through his hair and stomped back towards the window. He was not as in control as Isla had expected.

"From what you know to be truth."

"I'm not sure I know that anymore." Calder stared out the window for a moment. Hendra stared at his back, and then he turned slowly, his face dark. "I do," he said, his voice low. It made the hairs on the back of Isla's neck stand at attention. "You know that she remembers, that she has seen all that happened that day."

"She lived through it—of course she knows what happened. You heard the recordings. You saw her at the hearing."

"Not your lies. Not your version for the people. What actually happened, and who was there. I have seen it."

Hendra shook her head, and he walked more slowly back towards the table. He was far more terrifying than when he had charged across the room moments before.

"I was there," he said. Isla could see he was very sure of that, but he couldn't remember it.

"No, you weren't," she said, her voice light, friendly. "You were changing."

"You did this because of what happened."

"We had talked about this before that day. It was an opportunity we couldn't miss. No one would know you weren't there." The Hendra was calm and smiling, as though talking down a madman.

"You expected us to win. You expected us to defeat them. Why would I not be there?"

"Because it was time for Kalli to disappear and Calder to take his place."

"You made that decision. You should have left me in the cavern."

Hendra's eyes widened. So, she hadn't believed that he remembered—that any of them could really remember where they'd been and what had occurred.

Calder sighed, his shoulders dropping, the strength slipping from him. "You should have left me dead."

Hendra was shaking her head as she stood. When she took a step towards him, Calder stepped back. "You weren't dead," she whispered, "and I couldn't leave you."

"Were there others you might have saved?" Gray asked, and Isla wondered why she hadn't asked that question herself.

"Only Isla standing in the middle of the carnage."

"Standing?" Isla asked.

"Shock, they said." Hendra gave a little shrug as though it weren't important. "There was so much damage, so much blood. They were as surprised in saving your arm as they were that you survived at all."

Isla ran her fingers over her arm where a scar had run not so long ago.

"They would have killed you if they could. They killed everyone else. They are the enemy, and yet you would work with them."

"You were to work with them as the Hendra, as the Complex had done for generations. Now you would destroy us all. You are the enemy of the Complex," Calder said, his voice too calm, too measured. Isla leaned away from the table.

"How dare you!" Hendra growled, leaping out of the chair. Calder took a small step forward, making Hendra flinch, and she sat back heavily. "I am going to save us all," she added, but her confidence appeared to have slipped a little.

Calder stood over her. "Not like this."

"I know what I'm doing. I know what they are."

"You don't," Gray whispered.

"You sound like the minister."

"He was here?" Gray asked.

"Came with his chief to try and tell me how to run the Complex."

"Did he ask after Alice?" Isla asked.

"Of course, he did. But it was part of his ruse. She is there—she has to be."

Isla sighed, and Gray rested his hand on her shoulder. "Would you rather destroy us all than work with the Rohendra?" she asked.

"I don't need to work with them—and I am removing them, not destroying the Complex."

"In removing them, you will destroy us all."

She shook her head. "There was a time before the Rohen, before the partnership, where my ancestors thought they ruled the stars and yet they were puppets. I am no such leader."

"The Rohen *are* the Complex," Isla insisted.

"No one could believe that."

"How can you think that you are the only one to know what is going on, that the world works the way you think it does?" Calder implored. "So many before you knew the truth; they may have shared that. I've seen children with more understanding of the universe than you." Calder's expression towards the Hendra reflected what Isla had seen too often herself.

"I know more than you. I've seen it. I've felt it."

He shook his head slowly. "I've seen it." He raised his finger to point at Gray, whose hold on Isla's shoulder tightened just enough. "Show her," he commanded.

"I can't," Gray said softly. "Not without the books."

"But you know the words. You know the history."

"It isn't as clear as the stories written in the books." Isla turned to look into his concerned face, and he shook his head. "It won't work."

"Tell her who she is," Isla suggested. "Tell her what she is to the Rohen."

Gray took a deep breath, but as he stepped out from behind her, the Hendra held up her hand.

"I'll not be told your stories. I know what I am. I know the histories. I don't need your version, your lies."

"I believe him," Calder said, and he gave Gray a subtle nod. "Tell her."

Gray closed his eyes and breathed out a word, similar to something Isla had heard before but one she couldn't have explained. A shimmering man appeared in the middle of the room, and the Hendra squealed. It was her father, younger, stronger, smiling.

"Show her the current Hendra," Isla whispered.

Gray murmured another word. The former Hendra disappeared to be replaced with a silver copy of the current Hendra. She looked stern, much as she did now, only more confident.

"Show me the next Hendra," Hendra demanded, and he whispered the name before Isla could suggest he wait. The young woman appeared, her uniform clear, the same shimmering silver of the illusion. Hendra stepped closer. She smiled as she lifted her hand to the young woman's face, her long straight hair pulled back in a low ponytail. A whisp had broken free and was blowing about her face, but when she smiled, she appeared to be looking towards Isla rather than the woman before her.

"You have proven with your tricks that I am not the destruction of the Complex."

"If they are tricks, then we have proven nothing," Calder said as the next Hendra faded and Hendra stepped forward into the space she had occupied.

"My child will follow me, and the Complex will endure."

"Only if you stop this," Isla said.

Hendra smiled that all-knowing, uncomfortable smile as she walked around behind her desk. She glanced at the space the next Hendra had taken up rather than at them and put her hand to a panel on the desk. "General?"

"I've lost him, Your Grace."

"It no longer matters," she said.

"Don't do this," Isla pleaded.

"Your Grace," came the reply, and then there was nothing.

Isla braced herself for the reaction, as though she would feel the wave of Urgway disintegrating from Rennet. She was certain she would feel something. Then Gray was holding her hand, his eyes closed as though he too was waiting for something they wouldn't miss in the aftermath of whatever it was Hendra had just approved.

They waited, nerves fraying by the second, and all the while she stood behind her desk grinning.

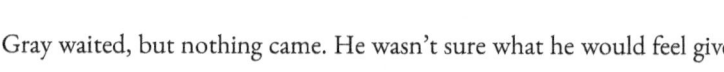

Gray waited, but nothing came. He wasn't sure what he would feel given the distance they were from Urgway, and yet he expected the planet's destruction to ricochet through the entire solar system.

"It is done," came the general's reply. Gray was relieved that the man, obviously still on the planet, had survived.

The relief was audible in Calder as well, as he sighed. Isla leaned into Gray as he closed his arm around her. It appeared she had expected the same.

And then the lights dimmed, and the sound of power leaving the room created a silence Gray didn't think he had heard before. Was he more attuned to the hum of the Rohen than he had previously realised?

There was a gentle knock on the door, and a young man appeared.

Hendra looked up at him, her smile still secure across her face as though she had won.

"I can't raise anyone," he stammered.

"What power do we have?" Hendra asked.

He shook his head and backed out of the room. Hendra put her hand back to the comms panel on her desk and then thumped at it. Isla pulled from Gray's hold and walked towards the window. The city shimmered in the light, glass reflecting the sunlight, and yet it appeared to be less brilliant. As though the shine had gone out of it.

"Well done," Isla murmured. "You might just have achieved what you wanted."

"Destroying the Rohen?"

"And with it the Complex," she said, turning back to Hendra.

Gray waited for the realisation to set in as to what had just happened. The extent of what Hendra's actions had caused.

"Rubbish," she snapped, sitting down at her desk. "If they are gone, we are still here and all the better for it."

"You can't communicate with your people. You can't use your technology."

"You can't travel," Calder said.

"I don't need to."

"How will you talk with your council? How will you ensure they do your bidding and don't take this chance to rule their planets as they see fit?" Isla asked.

Hendra's smile slipped just a little. "They hold too much respect for me to do such a thing." But there was a waver to her voice as though she didn't quite believe it.

"And your greatest ally is trapped far away." Calder crossed his arms.

She looked at him with apparent confusion, as though he were that man, but Gray doubted Calder would do as directed by her now. She had achieved what she wanted and lost the Complex as she'd been told she would.

"This is just a power issue, and not necessarily connected to Urgway."

Gray looked at Isla as she closed her eyes. He wondered if she would leave him here, or if she was searching for the Rohen. She stood still for far too long, and he stepped forward and rested a hand on her shoulder.

"They are gone," she whispered. "Was it their choice?"

Is she not sure, or is she hopeful the Rohen will return? he wondered.

"You can feel the loss," Calder said, his voice low and kind.

"It is a power outage. I will not be led by your attempts to convince me this has destroyed the Complex." She put a hand to her belly and sat down slowly, her face pale. Calder stepped forward, almost worried, as though he needed to check on her and the welfare of the child, but he couldn't quite bring himself to go to her. She wasn't what she had pretended.

But Gray understood that no matter what she had turned out to be, there was a connection between the two of them and it would influence whatever Calder did next. Hendra winced, and the large soldier moved closer to her.

"The child is Rohendra," Isla whispered, as though she too might be in danger. But Gray had seen her grown, knew that she would become something great and therefore would survive this. Despite his telling Isla that there was no way for him to see the future, for he couldn't, the Rohen had a sense of what was to come and how it would come about. They knew of the child, and they had shown him the word for her as Hendra.

"She also feels the loss," Gray whispered, sure now that what the Rohen had shown him was the truth.

"I don't feel any loss," Hendra snapped. "The child just moves a little more vigorously."

"Hendra understands what you have done," Gray continued. He wanted to use her name, her real name, the one provided by the Rohen, but something made him hesitate. Something he wasn't sure of, that he would have the chance to use it in the future, but that it would only put her in danger if he used it now. If he exposed what she was to the woman who kept her safe.

The Hendra glared at him. Calder glanced to the side and stopped his forward motion.

The secretary raced into the office again, then stopped and took in the stillness around him. "I have tried to reach the general but cannot. A soldier has gone to the Elite, but nothing is working."

"Something is working," Hendra murmured, looking back towards the door as Minister Burre strode in. He looked disappointed. Gray stepped back, hoping that disappointment was aimed at him.

"Not as you would wish it." His voice was low and level, but it made Gray step back again. He hadn't heard anything like anger from this man in the short time he had known him, but he could feel it ebb from him now as he made his way across the room.

"What right do you have to come here?" she demanded.

"A greater authority than you have sent me."

"There is no greater authority. Not now."

The minister shook his head.

"You were to stop this," he said, turning to Isla who hung her head.

"It is not her fault. We tried, but it was for Hendra to learn that this was a mistake. She had to be the one to end it. She could not see the..." Calder stopped.

Gray was somewhat surprised that he had not only agreed this was the reason behind it but supported the notion.

"I understand," the minister said, bowing his head to Calder.

"What exactly were you doing while you were away with these people?" Hendra demanded.

"Learning the truth," Calder returned quickly, and she paled further.

"Their truth," she murmured, as though that might be different from what she had told him. But as much as he had seen the truth, Gray had thought Calder still had not accepted it. Hadn't he given Kalli up for dead long ago?

"I was there," he snapped.

Gray was tempted to take another step back. The cold, calculating man who had tormented them for so long reappeared before him, only his hatred was aimed at the woman he had supported until recently.

Hendra opened her mouth and then closed it as she ran her hand over her belly. Gray thought he could see a wave of movement, although he doubted that was the case.

"I was in the middle of the attack, the one we should not have started, the one we should not have pursued."

"They were threatening to take over the Complex. They had to be stopped, and I thought we could..."

"You had no idea what they really were, what power they had and what it would do. Or did you?" he asked, something wary in his voice and something dangerous. "Did you know just what we could face?"

"There was a risk," she admitted, although she had yet to admit the truth of sending him in. "But you were the best we had."

Calder's face set into something very dark. Gray felt the world tip just a little, marking this as a moment he would never forget.

"Why did you bother to lie?"

"Because more than that girl should have walked out of that cavern."

"Do you know what was in there?" Isla asked.

"Rohen. It was all I needed to know."

Isla seemed to relax somewhat. When Gray looked to the minister, he shook his head once. Hendra had been guessing, working with limited knowledge and endangering them all.

"What did your father tell you?" Gray asked.

"It no longer matters."

"Of course it does. Whatever his words were to you, meant to pass on the knowledge of the Complex, they caused you to work against it."

"I have only ever worked for the Complex," Hendra said.

"Your version of it—your self-serving version of it," Calder muttered.

"How can you say that?"

"You sent me in to die! I believed I was doing as you needed me to do to help you save the Complex, but it was never about that. It was never a way for us to help everyone. It was only a way to ensure your rule."

"My rule was never in doubt. I am Hendra. I was destined to rule the Complex since before I was born."

"And yet you felt threatened and had to push others out."

"They would use it for their own purposes."

"They *are* the Complex," Isla whispered from her place by the window. "They are the reason we are all here. You didn't want to take control from them—you wanted to destroy them completely without considering what that would do."

"They would never truly share it. My father was sure in his dying breaths that they would take it for themselves and allow us to perish."

"They always had control. They didn't need to take it. In separating them, you have done far more damage. You have ended it all."

"Ended what?" Hendra demanded. "We are here."

"Without power and who knows what else."

Hendra looked around the room; it was becoming darker as the sun set. Gray half expected bombs to continue going off around the city, but they weren't needed now. It was all too late.

"It no longer matters," Calder said, looking at the minister. "She doesn't understand what she is, or what she has done."

"But can it be undone?" Isla asked.

The minister slowly shook his head.

"They knew what they were sending us into," Isla pressed. Gray agreed. The Rohen had known the outcome to this long before anyone else in the room was aware of it. They were never going to succeed against the Hendra. He wondered what the Rohen had hoped they would find. He looked at Isla, wondering if she had doubts as to what their role in all of this was. So far, it didn't appear to be very much—and they hadn't succeeded with any of it.

"There is a plan," he said, looking to the minister. The man barely raised his eyes, but the nod was there. He knew what was to come and, as Gray wanted to do, he trusted them to be right.

"No longer," Hendra said, standing and taking in the room. Her earlier uncertainty appeared to have gone, and her hand no longer rested on her belly.

"The world is not as you think," the minister repeated.

"What exactly are you minister of?" she asked, looking over the older man as though seeing him for the first time. She would have known him for years given his connection to Alice.

"Rohendra," he said. She opened and then closed her mouth. "I am their conduit to the chiefs and to the children of Rohendra. I know their will."

"And so you know I am right."

"You are far from right. Your father understood. The Hendra before him understood. And yet you think you can do differently and expect better for the Complex. The Rohendra are the Complex."

She shook her head again.

"The Rohendra are the Complex," he repeated and turned back towards the door.

Twenty

Isla followed the minister from the room and was surprised that she couldn't feel the Rohen despite walking into the forest rather than the hallway. The sun was bright after the dimmed office, and she leaned into the nearest tree.

"Is there a way to undo this?" Calder asked. She glanced at him, surprised that he had followed or been taken along with them. But then, the Rohendra were so sure he would help.

None of them had done enough to help stop this. Gray walked away from them, out through the trees. As tempted as she was to follow him, she knew he needed the space.

"Alice will have prepared dinner. Come inside," the minister said.

Isla nodded slowly, and Calder hissed a comment under his breath.

"She didn't poison her," Isla said. The minister ignored him and followed a different path from the one Gray had followed.

Calder's hand closed around her arm. As she looked up at him, he removed it quickly. "Maybe she had good reason," he muttered, stepping away from her.

"Maybe she was doing something else," Isla suggested.

"I'm sorry," he murmured.

"You were following orders," she replied, hoping it was what he had done. He was a soldier, after all.

"Not always," he added softly. "Since..." He indicated his face and then ran his hand through his short hair.

"She had faith in you to do what was needed."

He nodded. "But I didn't know."

Isla returned the nod and turned for the house. There would be a plan, a way to undo this, only she wasn't sure what it was. As she ran her hand over the bark of the trees, she felt sad for the forests lost. She had expected to feel that loss here and was surprised that she didn't. Calder's hand closed around her arm again, and he pulled her closer.

"I didn't want you dead," he whispered. She tried to see the man she'd known before in him, but she wasn't sure who he was now.

"You certainly tried hard for someone who didn't want it."

He released his hold then, but continued to stand close. "She should have let you go."

"Why did she wait so long?"

"She had begun to worry you would remember. I don't know what triggered her change in mind."

"She never worried that you would," Isla said, surprised by the flash of hurt that crossed his face.

He gave her a sad smile, stepped back and bowed his head. "Just a stupid soldier," he muttered, turning towards the house.

"She never thought that," Isla said, "or she would never have pulled you out."

As he continued to the house, she tried to reconcile the man before her with Kalli and Calder and could no longer work him out.

Isla was tempted to head for the library in search of Gray once they reached the house, but she knew he was out in the trees somewhere. She was surprised at the silence as she followed the minister into the dining room, where the children were sitting unmoving at the table. Despite the understanding of the Rohen and that it was here, the children appeared to sense far more than she had thought them capable of, even if they were gifted.

Calder sat in the nearest seat and looked them over while the minister sat at the head of the table. Isla remained standing. Calder looked up as Alice appeared beside her at the table, carrying a bowl that she added to the many already set before them. No one made a move to eat.

Isla waited for the harsh words or attack to come, but he too looked back to his empty plate as though he felt the loss of the Rohen.

"Is it really gone?" he asked, as though these people would have a better understanding.

They had heard the general, after all. Maybe the planet remained, the Rohen safe, and the communication was all that was gone. Isla turned back for the door, determined to find the answers to that herself and go to Urgway. She chastised herself that she had waited this long before thinking of it. But Alice took her arm and shook her head.

"Have you seen it?" Isla asked.

Alice shook her head and directed Isla with significant force towards a chair.

"I can't eat," she muttered.

"None of us can," Beth whispered.

"And yet you will," Alice said, remaining standing at the end of the table, her arms crossed. "All of you need to eat to maintain your strength so we can determine how to fix this."

"We can't fix what is gone," another child said as they ran a hand under their nose.

"That is why we are here," Alice chastised. "That is why we have come together and why we are safe here in the forests."

"Are the forests gone?" Isla asked, but Alice didn't acknowledge that she had spoken. She only focused on the children around the table.

"I can't see," Beth whispered, and Calder reached out to wrap a strong arm around the child beside him. The movement surprised Isla almost as much as the child, who then leaned into him as she began to cry.

"It will come," the minister said, staring across the table. He lifted a spoon from the nearest bowl and dropped its contents onto his plate. Although he then took hold of his fork, he didn't taste the food before him.

"Eat," Alice demanded. They moved through the motions of serving and eating the food, although Isla was sure that none of them actually tasted it.

She glanced through the large window, wondering where Gray was in the forest and whether he would return soon. They had been on the move for so long that none of them had the chance to eat or sleep properly for days.

"He's fine," Alice said softly as she sat beside Isla. "He has a greater understanding."

"Like you do?" Calder asked, his voice low as he scooped food onto Beth's plate.

Alice looked to her father then. "I have always done as was necessary."

"Do you want to explain the child?" Calder asked.

She shook her head, and Isla wondered just what Alice had done. She thought she understood why the Rohen had played some part in it. If they hadn't, then there wouldn't be another Hendra.

"Would you have carried the woman's child?" Isla asked her, but Alice maintained her focus on Calder and Beth. "Or was that never an option?"

"It was complicated."

"Was there not a man that you could have employed to make it less so?"

Alice looked at her with some degree of curiosity as she shook her head. "It was the only way."

Isla knew Alice believed that, but she wasn't sure it was true. She wondered if the Rohen had been manipulating more than Hendra when they'd implemented such a plan.

"Will she learn from you here?" Isla asked.

The minister looked at her as though only just considering the possibility. "That will be up to her mother."

"She hasn't had much choice so far in her child's wellbeing."

"Hendra?" Alice asked. "She will not be the mother," she said, looking at her father, but he gave a slight shake of his head.

"Again, there is more that the Rohen do that we do not understand," Isla murmured.

"We understand," Beth said. "And whether we agree or not"—she pushed back and looked up at the man beside her—"we follow because we know it is for the best of the Complex."

"Or is it best for the Rohen?" Calder asked her.

"The Rohen is the Complex," she said, scrunching up her face as though she couldn't understand why he didn't know that.

"For the continued sustainability of the Complex, the Rohen understand what needs to be done." Isla looked up at Gray standing in the doorway. He looked far worse than she thought she felt. "We might not agree with it. We may not see the sense in it, but it is what is necessary, and they have always been willing to do what is necessary."

"And that is what Hendra thinks she is doing, the reason she might have just blown away a whole planet," Calder said.

"Did she?" Gray asked.

"She will never understand," Beth whispered. "She is too hidden from the world in her office."

Calder stood, the movement quick, and several of the children at the table flinched.

"That is not a good idea," the minister warned as Calder's face grew dark. Isla stood slowly, glancing at Gray, and a tired smile formed on his lips.

"But it might be all we have. She needs to understand what she is—what her part in the world is," Isla said.

Calder nodded as Isla reached for his hand, and Gray wrapped his arms around her.

It had seemed like a crazy idea, but when Calder looked at Gray, he knew it was something they could do to try and fix this. He had only ever been doing what he thought he should to benefit the Complex, but in a very short time he had come to understand that he was only doing it for the good of the Hendra.

She needed to understand who she was and what they could do for the benefit of all. The image of the shimmering woman who would be their next Hendra filled his senses. Although she didn't exist yet, there was something about her, a different kind of strength he knew they needed in the position of Hendra.

He breathed out slowly as Hendra looked up from her desk and then stood, focusing on the small group before her.

"What in the name of the stars are you doing?" she snapped, but there was something nervous about her. "Where did you go?"

"It doesn't matter," Calder said. His hand still tight in Isla's, he reached for the woman standing behind the desk. She was too slow to react, and he closed his hand around her arm. "All that matters is where we are going."

There was a sharp intake of breath as the world darkened around them, making him wonder at the light that had been in her office.

"Isla?" he asked as she let go of his hand.

"There is nothing here I can pull from," Isla said.

"Where are we?" Hendra asked.

"Urgway," Gray answered.

"Still here then?" Hendra snapped, her tone sarcastic.

"But little else, it seems," Isla murmured.

"Where is the general?" Hendra asked.

Calder reached for Isla again, hoping she would take them to him or find some light as the dark grew heavy around them. A strange fear grew in his chest, and he thought he could see swords or flashes of silver in the light of the dusters. Faces appeared. Faces he had known flashed around him, damaged and dead, and then he was falling. He focused on Isla's fear as she looked around her. He couldn't reach her—it was too great a distance between them, and there was nothing left.

He cried out, but no one answered. The silence was stifling. A hand rested on his arm, and he screamed.

"Kalli," Isla whispered, "it is safe."

"Is it?" he asked too quickly, then realised he had let go of the Hendra.

"They aren't here," Isla said, "and they wouldn't hurt you now."

"Are you certain of that?" Hendra's voice asked, further away than he expected.

"Yes," Isla responded, her voice certain.

"If they weren't," Gray said, his voice low but echoing around them, "they would not have sent us to you."

Calder was sure the Rohen had sent Isla, but where one went so did the other. "Can you take us out of here?" he asked.

"Not right now," Isla said. "Find a seat and we'll see what can be seen in the morning."

"What if she escapes?" he asked, thinking of the Hendra.

"There is nowhere to go."

Twenty-One

Hendra blinked into the dim light, surprised by the debris surrounding her. How she had managed to move through the space at all in the dark without breaking an ankle or her neck, she didn't know. Half the ceiling appeared to have collapsed onto the floor between her and the other members of the group that had dragged her here. She still didn't understand how that had happened. Did Calder have some skill she wasn't aware of? Was he another spy of the Rohen, working against her while appearing to be her only ally?

"Has she been there the whole time?" he was asking Isla, and although Hendra didn't know who he was talking about, she could guess.

"Alice is hiding with her father," Hendra called across the space.

"She has work to do," Gray said.

Hendra watched him as she stood slowly. How had this man been able to win over the woman and soldier? But then, they were all connected. He had helped Isla escape from Calder; he had known Calder as a boy and then on the Sparrow. Was that the reason he had lived this long? Calder was supposed to kill him when they had returned them to the facility. But the other sparrow had died while this one survived. She looked between the three of them and then back around the space.

It was a cavern somewhere underground, she suspected, looking at the ceiling. The great chunks of rock that had been knocked free now littered the ground around them. There was no sign of the Rohen, or anything else that would indicate they had been here. She had never ventured into the caverns before, although this was where she would have met with them at some long-distant point. She had sent in an army instead to annihilate them.

She looked over the three talking again.

"Is this where it happened?"

"No," Calder said without looking back at her.

Despite the fact that they were in a cavern, there was light. And so there must be light coming in. There must be a way out. She made her way carefully towards the wall of the cavern, working around the rough boulders and trying not to trip over the smaller chunks of rock that covered the ground. When she reached the wall, she ran her hand over the rough stone, looking for an exit. Her fingers found the crevice before her eyes did, and she wondered at it. Stretching from the floor up and across the wall and across the domed ceiling, it passed through the place were some of the larger rocks had fallen.

Light seeped in through the crack. Something creaked, and she pressed her back into the rough surface. "This isn't safe," she muttered.

"No," Isla said, looking up at the ceiling with her. "It is likely to come down soon."

"Then get us out!" Hendra demanded. The stupid girl had gotten them into the cavern in the first place.

"I can't," she said with a shrug of one shoulder.

"Why not?"

"Because I use the Rohen to travel," she said, walking towards Hendra, who wanted the wall to open up and allow her to escape. "There is no Rohen, and that is your fault."

"There must have been Rohen to let you carry all of us here." She stopped and squinted at the woman. "You aren't going to tell me anything, are you?"

"Who knows what you might do with the information," Calder muttered.

"It isn't like I can reach anyone to tell them," she returned. "I can't raise anyone—we can't get out. We will all likely die here."

"You won't," Gray said, his voice low and disappointed.

"You want me to die?" she asked, more hurt by the idea than she thought she could be. Who were these people to decide whether she should live or die?

"Your child will protect you," Calder replied for him. "If they know the child is here. As there is no Rohen, they may not be able to save you."

"What do they care for my child?" Hendra snapped, but as she looked at the stern features on the girl, she remembered her saying something of the child being Rohendra. Her hands closed around her belly. They would not die here. She would make sure of that.

"They gave you what you always wanted, what you needed to maintain your place as Hendra. All you have wanted to do is destroy them. They will protect you, for whatever that information is worth." Isla crossed her arms. The anger of her words was evident in her whole body.

"You think you can manipulate me to get what you need from this."

"What we all need from this situation," Isla said too calmly, "is for the Complex to continue. You can see what you have done to Urgway. This is one small part. Until we can find a way out onto the surface of the planet, we have no idea just what is left, and who," she added quietly. Hendra wondered if Isla was thinking of something else. Another part of her life Hendra had taken away, or at least allowed Calder to take. It had surprised her to some degree that he would go to such lengths, but he had done far worse and rarely needed her direction regarding what was needed.

Although he appeared to be looking to someone else for that direction now.

"How do we get out?" Hendra demanded. "Do we wait for you to decide you are willing or for the roof to collapse?"

"You won't likely survive that," Calder muttered, but he was looking at the others when he spoke. Did he no longer care if she survived?

"How quickly your allegiance shifts," she growled.

"My allegiance is where it always was." He turned a bright smile on her, which made her step back. "For myself and my survival."

She shook her head. Could he really only care about himself? Maybe that was how he had survived that day. If only just. He wasn't trying to protect Isla or they would have been found closer together. Knowing that the Rohen had tried to kill her, why was she so willing to support them now?

"I don't understand," she admitted.

"No," Isla said firmly, "and you don't appear to want to understand. I had thought showing you how the world looks now that you have gone against your duty would have some impact. But there is nothing I could show you that would change your thinking."

"I don't need to change my thinking," Hendra said. She wanted to snap at Isla, but who was the girl really in all of this to tell her how to run the Complex? She had been doing it long enough. "They didn't give me this child," she said, trying to dispel the thoughts this girl had tried to put into her mind. "He did." She indicated Calder with her chin.

He shook his head, and she took a step towards him.

"It is your child," she repeated.

"It was never mine. It belongs..." He took a breath. "She belongs to the Rohendra."

Hendra was surprised he'd used the word to describe them, as though admitting they were what Isla claimed. The girl gave him a sad look, and he nodded once in her direction. She had told him that then—she had convinced him that the child couldn't be his. And despite Hendra's vow to herself that she would never share the information with anyone, she knew it was his child. He was the only one who could do what no one else could.

"Alice could have carried a child, but the technology is not as reliable as the traditional methods," Hendra said—not that she had to explain herself to these people, but she needed Calder on her side. She was struggling to understand why he wasn't. One lie in all that time. Or was this the lie he had referred to?

"She would not have," Isla answered as though she would know Alice's mind. But then perhaps she did—perhaps they'd been colluding long before Hendra's wife had tried to disappear. There was too much that she didn't understand, and it was both frustrating and frightening. She sank down to the floor. Although Calder took half a step towards her, he didn't come to see if she was well—if their child was well.

"You can't kill me," she said.

"We don't want to kill you," Calder said, his arms crossed as though to put a further barrier between them. "I want you to understand what you have done."

"*You* do?" she asked, looking at the woman standing back and the sparrow now silent.

"Yes. It is my Complex too, and you have used me to cause it harm when I only wanted to work to save it."

"How did I do that?" she asked as something creaked above her head and dust drifted down over her. She scurried forward to stand in the group, as though that might keep her safer.

"You sent me in to die."

They had been over that, hadn't they? Hendra couldn't think clearly here. She needed to be in her office, surrounded by her security, her secretaries and the information she usually had at her fingertips. Although she wasn't sure she could have that now.

"Take me to the surface," she demanded.

Isla nodded and stepped forward, putting her hand to her arm, and Hendra squeezed her eyes closed. The hot sun burnt her skin. She squinted into the sky, lifting an arm to shield her from the heat, only it had little effect.

"This does not prove there is nothing left of Urgway," she said, glancing around her while squinting into the bright light. They were standing in the middle of a desert. The red sand stretched out around her, but there was nothing close. In the distance, she could see the haze of mountains—or was it an illusion produced by the heat on the surface?

"Where do you think we are?" Isla asked.

"In the middle of the desert. If this had occurred at the time of the mines closing, then the general would not have been able to call me."

Isla tilted her head to the side, and Gray and Calder shared a look. Did she think Hendra should have referred to it as anything else?

"And if the Rohen were gone, you would not have been able to bring me here."

Calder sighed. "Give her back. It isn't worth the effort."

Isla bowed her head, reaching for Hendra, but she stepped out of her reach.

"You can stay here if you prefer," Isla said.

"You wouldn't do that to my child. You know she is important, and you would help the Rohen keep her safe."

"They may come for you," Isla said, stepping back. "They may not after this. Maybe they'll just start again, and the image of the Hendra Gray showed you was someone else entirely."

Hendra hadn't considered that, and yet she had seen something so familiar in the woman who had glimmered before her—the eyes that had belonged to her father. She knew the woman, knew the girl, knew without doubt that the image had been her daughter.

But she didn't trust that the Rohen would save her. Even if they thought they were involved with the child who would become the next Hendra. She would pretend to work with the girl for now, but when it came to it, she would ensure the next Hendra was well aware of just what the Rohen were and what she would need to do.

The Rohen were sparse in the air, but Isla could feel them in the sand beneath her feet. She knew they had hidden themselves further from sight with the destruction of the mines rather than be destroyed with it. It would take time for them to trust to return. She reached for Hendra then, understanding that there was no change in her. No matter what she tried, Hendra would only believe as she wanted to, and this would not end how Isla hoped.

She rested her hand on Hendra's arm. They were still standing in the sun, only it was overlooking the mine Hendra was so sure the general was still at. The tall structure over the mine was bent and twisted; the ground appeared to have opened up, and part of the landing pad had disappeared into a sinkhole. The buildings had collapsed. Some of them had disappeared beneath the ground as well. Isla wondered if that had happened long after the general had left or at the time of the explosion.

Calder had guessed at what might occur, and he had been right. Isla was still surprised that there was any of the planet left at all, but as the ground rumbled beneath her feet, she wondered how long it would last.

"Is he in there?" Hendra asked.

"Who?" Calder asked.

"The general."

"Long gone—likely headed back to the city. If there is a city to return to."

The ships were gone, but that didn't mean they had flown out. The communications weren't working, but that didn't mean everything had stopped. Or did it? It had certainly appeared that way at Hendra Central. If the Rohen were unwilling to assist with anything the people needed, and if that was to convey their importance without giving away what they were, then it was a good plan.

Although considering the mess before her and the sense of danger she'd had in the mine, Isla still felt an uncertainty for Urgway's future. There were many more than just the general and his soldiers on the planet, and they couldn't all be hidden in the forests beneath the ground.

"Isla?" Gray asked, resting his hand on her arm. She looked up into his concerned face.

"I'm relieved it is here," she said. "But I don't know that it is enough." She thought of the silence around the table at the minister's home. The children had felt far more than they had said, had felt a loss. Did any of them really understand what was to come? She glanced at Calder, who had comforted Beth. What had she seen or understood that Isla hadn't allowed her the time to explain? "I keep thinking that this comes back to Hendra, but perhaps she isn't where we need to be focused."

"You should be focused on the Rohen," Hendra said, lifting her hand to try and block the sun, sighing as she did so.

Isla pulled a scarf from the air, similar to the one Gray had given her long ago, and held it out to her. Hendra eyed it suspiciously but took it.

"Maybe you are right," Isla said. "Maybe the only way forward is in the Rohen." She looked back towards the mine and wondered at the forests beneath the surface. In a heartbeat, she left the others standing on the ridge and was amongst the trees where, whether by design or accident, they had nearly taken her life. Large rocks had fallen from the walls and ceiling of the cavern, but it was still intact. The trees glowed a little, and the fungi at their base glowed more brightly.

She stepped forward and pressed her hand to the nearest tree. She wished she had Gray's word to make it shine brighter as she made her way into the forest. It smelt of home and yet not at the same time. Some branches had been knocked down with some of the rocks, but the damage was minimal.

"What of the others?" she asked. "She didn't do as she threatened?"

"We are still here," a deep voice vibrated through her, and the world seemed to tilt with it. The ground beneath her feet vibrated with another force.

"For how long?"

"She has done as she wanted. She has almost succeeded in removing us from the world." A silver figure moved out from behind a tree, and Isla's relief was instant at the sight of the humanoid form.

"You are still here. The trees are still here."

"But not for long. We may not be able to wait for the child."

"What can I do? She won't listen to me. I can't make her understand what she has done and what she needs to do for the good of the Complex."

"Is it only for the Complex you ask?"

Isla took a step back, bumping into a tree. "Of course," she said.

"Not for yourself or those you wish to protect?"

"In saving the Complex, I would save those I want to protect," she stammered. She didn't really have anyone. She cared for the Rohen in some way, and Kalli, but Gray was the only one she really cared for—and he wouldn't care for her if she sacrificed anyone for him. "I have only done as you have asked of me."

"What would you do if the other forests were in danger?"

"Are they?" she asked.

"With Hendra, they are all in danger of being lost along with the rest of us."

Isla knew that. It was why she was working with the Rohen as she was, to help protect the whole Complex. Hendra was the threat. She was the reason it was in such a position, and she had to understand that to stop what she was doing. But Isla couldn't make her understand, and she could not see another way.

The being before her tilted their head a little to one side. It appeared they were trying to read her.

"What other option is there?" Isla asked. "To protect the queen, we have to protect the Hendra as well."

The being before her disappeared, and she sank down to the forest floor. What else could she do?

"I have done as you have asked," she whispered to the tree. "I found the containment, I worked with Calder, I tried to save Kalli. She will destroy it and you, and there will be nowhere for the next Hendra to grow."

She looked up into the branches above, wanting to climb up and see what was there—or maybe just to hide away amongst the leaves and let someone else try to find an answer to all of this.

Something the minister had said about the next Hendra came back to her. That it would be up to her mother. But did that mean they would find a way to work with her, that she would support them? Hendra herself was certain the Rohen couldn't be trusted, and Isla knew there was nothing she could do that would change her mind.

Twenty-Two

Hendra squealed, and Gray looked back from the ruin of the mine. He had been trying to guess at where Isla had gone and how long before she returned. A soldier stood with a duster pressed into Hendra's back, and Calder grinned too easily.

"Take off the scarf," Calder muttered. Hendra raised her arms slowly and lowered the scarf.

The soldier staggered back and dropped to his knees. "I am sorry, Your Grace, I did not recognise you. How did you get here?" He looked up at her.

"Where is the general?" she demanded, pulling the thick material back up over her head to shield her from the sun.

Gray rubbed at his forehead; he longed for the same. Although it wasn't as hot as he remembered, it was a constant heat, and there was no relief from it. How long until Isla returned?

"He headed towards the city, Your Grace. We are ensuring no one tries anything." He indicated the group, and Gray warily watched the soldiers moving in around them. They had been prepared for the climate, at least. He wondered if any of them would be willing to share a cloak.

"Who is left to try anything?" Calder asked.

The soldier leapt to his feet and snapped a salute for the colonel. Gray turned back to the mine.

"We shall escort you," the soldier offered.

"There is no need," Calder answered. Gray wondered if he would wait for Isla to return.

"How far is the city?" the Hendra asked.

The soldier opened his mouth and then closed it, looking to Calder for confirmation.

"Days on foot. We'll wait," Calder murmured.

Gray felt the relief of Calder's words. Heading out into the desert unprepared would be a dangerous idea.

"What happened to the ships?" Calder asked.

The man shook his head. "They were gone when we came out. We assumed they fell into the hole."

"You didn't," Calder said.

"We lost men in this mess, Colonel."

Calder gave him a short nod and came to stand by Gray. "Do you think she will return?"

"She didn't get what she wanted," Hendra said behind him, but Gray didn't turn to look at her. "She is likely sulking."

"Isla doesn't sulk," Gray said, but she did feel things deeply. She had tried so hard to stop this and, despite the relief at the planet still being there, the damage was significant. He didn't know how deep it ran. There were sinkholes here, but what was the rest of Urgway like? Had large cracks made it to the centre of the planet? Was Reilly's family safe? He needed Isla so he could check on them. It would take him weeks to walk that far. He started towards the mine, and Calder caught his arm.

"You got any spare cloaks?" he grumbled.

"Sir," a soldier at the back of the group called. He pulled a pack from his back, rummaged through it and then stood before Calder with two cloaks in his hands. Calder took one, shook it out and handed it to Gray, then did the same with the second one, which he wrapped around his shoulders and up over his head. He waved the soldier away without thanks.

"She will return," he said, his voice low. "You two have a way of finding each other."

Gray nodded once, but he wasn't sure. Isla wasn't as clear on this as she had been previously.

"The colonel doesn't make decisions for me," Hendra growled. "We will start towards the general."

"Your Grace," a soldier said, his voice a little shaky.

"I will leave you here," she said.

"We'll find you once Isla returns," Gray said without turning around. She had to know that she couldn't have it all her way. Not now.

The damage to Urgway was not as severe as he had first imagined, but it was immense. As they looked over the destruction before them, he knew she had disappeared somewhere beneath the surface. It wasn't safe, and without the Rohen he was worried there was a serious chance he could lose her this time.

"I would like out of this heat," Calder muttered, pulling the cap of the cloak further over his face.

Gray nodded, but he couldn't take his eyes from the mine. "Do we follow or do we stay?"

"I didn't think you would leave, but then she would find you anywhere."

"You said that already," Gray muttered, not turning to look at the man. He suspected some level of jealousy, but he wasn't ready to see it on his face.

"You belong together."

Gray turned. Calder's face was shielded somewhat from view by the cape.

"I'm serious. I admit there was something annoying about the two of you teaming up. But there seems to be something else now, something I can't come between."

"Do you want to?" Gray asked, more sharply than he intended.

Calder shook his head and looked beyond him. "She's underground, isn't she?"

"Likely, yes."

"Have you seen this?"

Gray shook his head.

"But you know the next Hendra to come."

"I understand the word already exists for her. Several words," he added softly as Calder moved a step closer.

"Why several? She will be Hendra and only Hendra."

"Not this one," he murmured, looking back out over the desert.

"What do you...?" Calder stopped as a large tearing noise filled the world and the leaning structure over the mine tilted slowly.

It appeared to fall in slow motion. Gray thought he could race down and catch it before it crashed to the red sand, but it hit the ground before he had taken a step. The following noise was almost as loud as the first, and the ground beneath crumbled away as though there wasn't solid rock beneath the surface. It disappeared with the sand, leaving an even bigger hole than before.

"Come on," Gray murmured. "Isla would have heard that—she would understand what was going on and the need to get out."

"Unless she thinks she can protect the trees," Calder said, his voice nearly lost to the crashing as the hole widened and what was left of the buildings slipped away.

"Others are protecting them," Isla said, wrapping her hands around Gray's arm. He was too frightened to look away from the madness before him. The ground beneath their feet rumbled and shook, and he feared they would disappear just as quickly.

"Where is Hendra?" she asked.

"Headed off to find her general," Calder said.

"Alone?"

Gray shook his head as he looked her over, worried she was injured in some way from the world tearing apart around them.

"She will be safe enough for the moment while we check on the nearest city. I want to see what damage has been done beyond the mine."

Within moments, they were standing on the outskirts of the city Gray recognised as where he had first met Isla. Where he had also followed her to stop her doing anything silly and then caught her leaping from an exploding building. The ground rumbled beneath his feet, but it was a quiet, distant noise.

Dust blew about them. Despite a desperate need to stand between the shelter of the buildings from the sun and where the air would be cooler, Gray was sure it too would come crashing down around them. He didn't want to get caught beneath another pile of rubble.

Isla's hand finally slipped into his. The wind continued to hurl dust, and the planet rumbled beneath his feet. There was no sound of people, no vehicles, no ships overhead, and no one that he could see.

"Where is everyone?" he asked.

"Where would you go?" Calder asked, and although it was stilted, he didn't sound cruel and accusing.

"Maybe a garage?" Gray suggested, looking down at Isla.

She shook her head, and he wondered if she was worried about her friends or if she doubted the dragonfly was on the planet anywhere. Calder had possibly long ago destroyed it.

"We do seem to travel by Isla much more efficiently," Calder murmured.

"The damage is not the same here," she said, squatting down and pressing her hand into the hot sand. She dragged her fingers through the crimson granules as another rumble moved through Gray.

"It might be soon. It has started what she wanted it to—the planet will break up."

"No," Isla said, standing. "I don't think it will."

Gray thought he saw movement ahead of them. Something silver flashed in the sun, and then it was gone.

"They are here," Calder whispered.

He must have seen it too. Isla stood, brushed the sand from her hands and headed into the city.

"What are you looking for?" Gray asked, catching her arm and slowing her down.

"A way to make her understand."

"She is never going to understand," Calder growled. "She is set on this."

"What do you think could make her understand?" Gray asked. "She has seen the same damage we have, and it has made no impact on her. She only thinks about the Rohendra being defeated."

"She sensed something with the child," Isla said, but she was looking ahead of them. Gray searched amongst the buildings, wondering if there was more there than he could see. Although Calder had just seen something of the Rohen, too.

"What do they want?" he asked.

She looked up at him. "The child. Hendra to stop."

"She doesn't believe the child at risk," Calder said. "Could you bring her here?"

"Is there something here she would want?"

Calder shrugged as though that wasn't what he cared for. Gray had the feeling that he was needing her close again, that there was a connection between them—between him and Hendra—and that he would try to save her in the end.

"I don't know that it is that easy," Isla said.

"You can form anything in the Rohen," Calder said, his voice smooth, and Gray wondered if he fully appreciated the skill she had or if it was a way for her to do as he needed.

"It wasn't that long ago that skill scared you," she said, heading into the space between the buildings. Although it made him nervous to do so, Gray followed.

"What could she do out there?" Gray asked as Calder remained in the sun, looking back out over the red desert that stretched to the horizon behind them.

"They won't let her die, will they?" he asked, more than a little worry in his voice.

"They will protect that child with all they have," Isla returned, still walking further into the city. She stopped and looked up at a newsstand, although the screen was black. Gray stepped up past her and tapped on the screen. Despite not being able to feel the Rohen as Isla did in the surroundings, the lack of it was palpable.

"I've never seen one like that," he said.

She shook her head. "They've gone," she said, turning away from the screen and heading along the cooler street.

Gray looked back from the screen to Calder, who was moving into the cool of the streets. Calder lowered his hood and glanced over his shoulder. Gray wanted to reassure the man that they would find the Hendra and that Isla could reach her before Calder demanded such a thing, if necessary. Although she didn't seem that worried that the leader of the universe was alone with a small group of soldiers in the desert of Urgway, with no way to reach anyone if they needed help.

"They will keep her safe," she said without turning, and Gray wondered what other skills—such as reading him—she had collected along the way.

"What is the plan?" Calder asked as he caught them up.

"I'm not sure there is one," Gray murmured.

"I needed to see what was here, what was left and where the people had gone. I'm not sure it will make any difference, and although I'm not as worried about the planet as I was, it is possible the people need something. That they aren't safe here."

"Is it worth evacuating the planet and leaving it for the Rohen?" Calder asked.

"How do we do that with no ships?" Gray asked.

"Are there no ships? Just because we haven't seen any doesn't mean there aren't any, or that they couldn't fly. The Rohen removed themselves—they could help if we asked. If Isla asked."

"They may not be willing, no matter how I ask. And I'm not sure I want to ask them for anything. I think we have taken enough."

"Have we taken or have they hidden?" Calder asked, the harsh, accusing tone that had been present before appearing to have returned. Gray was keen to remove him from the planet and far away from Isla.

"Where do you want to be?" he asked her.

"In the cool shade of the forest," she murmured, then smiled up at him. "But we need to see what has happened here, and what might follow."

"How far behind us are the general and his troops, do you think?"

"Too far to be any threat," Calder returned.

"Is he a threat to you?" Gray asked. "And what of the new advisor?"

"Where is he?" Isla asked, stopping and turning back to Calder. "He wasn't around when the bombs went off."

"He didn't appear to be the type to stick around when things got tough."

"You didn't even know him," Isla said.

"I know everyone. It was my job to know—what everyone could offer the Hendra, what they might want from her and what threat they could be."

"Everyone?" Isla asked again. A sharp edge had crept into her voice, and Gray wondered at what she was hinting.

"You didn't remember," Calder murmured, pushing past her then and walking further along the deserted street.

If there were no ships, or at least no Rohen to help the people leave the planet, how were there no hints of people now? Maybe beyond the next block of buildings, the world was a different place. He pulled at Isla, trying to get her to stop her exploring.

"It is fine," she murmured, and again he wondered about the readers. She smiled. "I am prepared for whatever we find."

"Are you?" he asked seriously. "I'm not sure I am."

She closed her hand around his and pulled him along, trying to keep up with Calder, who strode ahead of them now. Gray wondered if he had found something or had an idea of what might be ahead of them.

But as they turned the corner, there was only another desolate street ahead.

Twenty-Three

Hendra knew that no matter what she wanted, she was going to have to rely on the support of others. She might even have to do as Isla wanted for now, to survive this. The crimson sand stretched out around them. Far to the left were ragged mountains, but she couldn't even guess at how far away they were. For the first time in her life, Hendra regretted not travelling more, as her father had suggested long ago. She had as a girl, meeting dignitaries and being the face of the universe for him when needed. But as an adult, and particularly as Hendra, she had not strayed far beyond the Hendra Central of Rennet. She hadn't needed to.

But now, lost and alone, despite the number of soldiers surrounding her, she regretted her lack of understanding of the real world. She had far more knowledge than most, and yet she hadn't understood what it was to stand in the hot sun and scorching sand of Urgway—hadn't understood just how desolate it truly was. She wondered what other planets offered, other than just the Rohen, and what her father might have made of this situation. She wished she had him for advice now. If only he had handed over the reins long before his death. Would that be something she could pass to her child? Would it be something she would want to do?

"How far ahead of us is the general?" she asked anyone who would answer her.

"A good day or so, and they are likely moving faster than us."

"Why would that be?" she asked.

The soldier looked to another rather than answering her question.

Because of me, she thought. Because she was older and slow, and a weak woman, and he wasn't willing to say that out loud. "Do you have water?" she asked.

He handed her his canteen without hesitation, and she took only a sip before handing it back. He nodded thanks. "Are you comfortable in the heat, Your Grace?"

"Hardly," she muttered, though she was well sheltered with the scarf Isla had created for her. "But I can manage. And I can walk faster. What will we do when night falls?"

"Camp where we are," he said. "We have enough supplies, and I doubt there is anything living out here that would eat us."

"Comforting," she murmured.

They continued in silence. After what felt like hours in the hot sun, they came across a mound of sand. At first, she thought it might be something coming out of the ground, but as they drew closer, she recognised it as a burial mound. One of the soldiers knelt at one end and dug through the fine sand, pulling out a metal disk. He nodded and put it back into the sand.

"Who is it?" she asked softly as they gathered together, bowing their heads for a moment before continuing on.

"Corporal Eaf," the soldier who had dug through the sand answered. There was a murmur through the group, but it wasn't a name she knew. Would her father have known everyone dedicated to working to keep him safe? Was it worth her time learning these people when they would just die anyway?

"I am sorry," she murmured, remembering her own recent loss, even if the woman hadn't died as she had feared.

The ground rumbled as though in reply, and the soldiers yelled and ran on. She tried to keep up, glancing back as the mound disappeared along with the soldier buried beneath it. A large fissure opened up along the ground behind them, the tearing sound overwhelming her. She stumbled, falling into the hot sand, her hands burning as she tried to push herself back to her feet. The soldiers were ahead of her, not one of them pausing to ensure she was keeping up or safe.

A hand closed around her arm and dragged her to her feet, but they held her still. She could hear the sand falling away into the new fissure like water into a waterfall, but the hand was steady. A soldier glanced back towards her, stumbled and stopped.

Another did the same, and she turned into the shining light reflected by the being beside her. She tried desperately to pull from its hold, but it wasn't letting go.

"What do you want?" she cried.

"You to be safe, my queen," he replied, although the face didn't move as it spoke. The sound travelled through her, hummed through her, and she clutched at her belly with her free hand.

The soldier nearest raised a duster, and she held out her hand. She knew that would not work on them; he was more likely to miss and kill her or her child. He didn't lower the weapon, but he didn't fire. The world had become silent around them, other than the sound of sand rushing into the abyss. She chanced a glance behind her at the world breaking up. The rumbling had stopped, as had the damage. Perhaps there was more damage than to just the mines. It appeared she had not destroyed the Rohen as she had hoped.

A feeling of helplessness rushed over her, as though she had failed and there was nothing left for her.

"You are still Queen," he whispered across her skin.

"Let her go," one of the soldiers shouted.

"You do not want her protected?" the figure asked, the sound separate and yet vibrating from it.

The soldier lowered his weapon.

"It isn't safe," she murmured, unsure if she was referring to the being beside her or the surface of the planet.

"No," he replied, although she wasn't sure it was a male. The figure was tall, humanoid, but gave nothing away as to its gender. Did they even have a gender? Were they all the same? "We are one," the voice hummed through her. "We are many."

Hendra had the strange feeling that she wasn't going to survive this. The panic closed in around her chest and if she could have, she would have dropped to her knees.

"Can you take me to Isla?"

The being turned its head a little to the side. But it made no sound or indication that it would take her anywhere. She glanced back over her shoulder at the large, dark, narrow hole that had appeared behind her. Isla was so sure that they would protect her no matter what she did, for the good of the child, and yet Hendra wasn't so sure about that now that she was in their hold.

"You are safe," she said.

A laugh emanated from it, washing over her, and yet it wasn't a relaxed, open sound—it was cruel and made the hairs on her arms stand to attention.

"You are not," he whispered, leaning in close, and the world cooled around her as it went dark.

———◄O►———

The world seemed to creak, the buildings appeared to lean and the ground rumbled beneath her feet. Isla wasn't sure what she was looking for. She wasn't sure what she needed to be sure that this planet wasn't being destroyed. She wasn't even sure why it was so important. The people appeared to have gone. The Rohen had protected themselves, despite the loss of the mines. And they had managed to look after the forests. That was something. She knew that if something had happened to the forests, the repercussions would be far wider reaching than if the planet had been lost.

The people could be rehomed on other planets, but the trees were an essential part of the balance of the solar system—of the Rohendra Complex—and tied to the Rohen. Why hadn't Hendra listened to her when she had tried to explain that?

She only hoped Hendra was being cared for by the soldiers in the desert. They understood who she was, even if Isla was tempted to leave her out there to die in the heat. The child was important. If she were in any real danger, then the Rohen would help her.

At another cracking sound, a hand closed around her arm and pulled her back. She almost tumbled at the sharp tug, but Gray had her tight in his arms as the building crashed down around them.

She blinked through the dust, Gray's arms tight around her, and someone pressed against her back. The two of them shielded her, and she wondered at them working together.

"I'm ok," she murmured, and Calder stepped back, brushing at the dust covering his uniform. Gray was a little slower to release his hold, looking her over seriously. He stared into her face for a sign that she might not be as well as she claimed.

"At least we know no one is here," Calder said, taking another step back. "If there were people here, they would be moving around."

"How did they get off the planet?" Gray asked.

"Maybe they didn't," Calder suggested. "Maybe they found somewhere safer."

"I'm worried the whole planet might break up still," Isla said, looking at the debris. "I thought it might be ok, but I'm not so sure looking at this now. The Rohen might have had a way to protect the trees, but if the planet is breaking up, are they able to stop that?"

"They can form walls to redirect tunnels," Gray offered.

"You can pull anything from the Rohen—they could surely create whatever they needed to protect the trees and the planet."

"I'm not sure they can."

"The rumbling has stopped," Calder said. "If we are going to try and find anything in this city, now would be the time."

"I don't even know what I'm looking for."

"You wanted to come here for a reason," Calder said, but his tone was still friendly. "You know them—you know what they need."

"They need the Complex to continue, just as we do," she said. She took a step over the rubble and then stopped, a strange feeling filling her. The Rohen had returned, she could sense it, she could feel it. And yet there was something different, something uncertain in the way it felt.

"They have Hendra," she whispered.

"Who does?" Calder asked.

"The Rohendra. They have saved her from the desert, only I'm not sure she is safe."

"You said she was the safest woman in the universe," Calder said, his voice laced with anger.

She looked at Gray, who shook his head once. "The child is the most important," she said.

"And that is why they will keep her safe."

"Until the child arrives."

"No," Calder said, heading back out towards the sand. It was Gray who caught him by the arm.

"You can't help her this way," he said.

There was something pleading in the way Calder looked at her when he turned back from the sand.

"I can't go against them," Isla said.

"I'm only asking that you keep her safe."

"She could do that herself," Gray murmured. "All she has to do is work with them."

"She won't," Calder said. "No matter what is at stake, she won't."

Twenty-Four

T he stark white room was silent. Hendra tried to sense the rumbling of the planet, but there wasn't any. She didn't know if they were somewhere still on Urgway or if the Rohen had been able to carry her far away, like Isla had the skill to do. She wondered then for the first time if Isla was even human. She had assumed her skills were related to her hummer ability, and Calder had claimed she had shown no skill at all when he had worked with her in the Elite. But then, he had also failed to tell her about the Rohen copy, and it might be that the girl wasn't a girl at all.

She blinked into the bright light, wondering where the Rohen had gone. If the silver figure had been Rohen—but she knew it was. Her father had told her they took many forms. Not only had it appeared before the soldiers, unafraid of being seen when she had thought them so secretive, it had appeared as the liquid metal she had seen in the containers in the laboratories.

She looked up at the tall, hooded figure before her, its hands tucked out of sight within long sleeves, its face hidden in the darkness beneath the hood. Was this another silver being, trying to look like something else?

The arms moved slowly upwards, and old hands were revealed as she stepped back. He pushed the hood back to reveal an old face. It could have been any old man, except for the unnatural height and the oddly solid silver eyes.

"Please sit, Your Grace," he said, his old voice strong. She sat back without thinking into a metal chair. It was warm and soft, although she had felt something mocking in the tone when he had said *Your Grace*.

"What do you want?"

"All that you do."

"The Rohen removed from the Complex."

He sighed, but stared her down. She blinked into the strangely solid silver eyes, unsure where they were looking.

"We are the Complex," he said.

"You are Rohen?"

"We are Rohendra," he said. "We are many. We are one."

"I have heard that before, and yet I don't understand what you mean."

"And that is why you have done as you have. It stops. You are caretaker; you are to ensure the Complex continues to thrive. You are not doing that."

"All I do is for the Complex," she said, straightening her back. Who were these creatures to question her?

"All you do is for you. We have given you what you wished for. In return, you were to help us."

"I never made such a deal." She stood up from the chair.

"Then we will take it back."

She didn't believe that they'd been responsible for providing her with the child she needed to ensure her place in the world, but her hand rested on her belly all the same. Despite her willing it to move, it wouldn't.

The old man before her grinned, his eyes unsettling as she couldn't tell where they were focused. She shivered.

"There are many who would protect me," she said, disappointed that her voice sounded as shaky as it did.

"I am sure there are," he said, looking around the room. Hendra followed his gaze, but there was no one there. Then she looked behind her, and more tall men in robes appeared. Had they always been there?

"Isla will back me," she said, hoping it was true. The woman had pulled her from Rennet, after all.

"Island knows her place in the Complex," he said, bowing his head and finally blinking those silver eyes. "She backs the queen."

"Yes," Hendra said, settling back into the chair. "She does."

Despite her finding it difficult to read the creature before her, his eyes appeared to rest on her belly rather than her face as his features softened. "She will be all we need her to be and more."

"She?" Hendra asked. "You talk of my daughter."

He bowed his head. "She is a child of the Rohendra."

"She is mine," Hendra said slowly as he shook his head. "She was always mine."

"Rohendra," he repeated.

"She will understand what she needs to be," Hendra said forcefully, standing again.

When he stepped forward, she stepped back and was surprised to find the chair had disappeared. "That will depend on her mother," he said.

"I..." She stopped. *Did he mean Alice?*

"She will help," he said, turning away. Hendra stepped forward.

"I will not give you what you want," she said. "It is mine."

"It was never yours," Isla said, appearing at the far end of the room, Gray and Calder a step behind. Hendra was more relieved to see Calder than she could voice. He would stand for her. No matter what this girl had promised him, what stories they told, he was still loyal.

"You must understand that," Calder said, unmoving behind her.

Hendra shook her head. Did no one understand what she was trying to do—what she needed to do to save them all? These creatures before her were not what they were believed to be.

"Bring your allies forward," the creature said, moving his arm around in an arc. The general appeared, dusty and tired, several soldiers with him;

Michaels and her new advisor appeared on the other side. They both stepped forward, eyeing the man before them. Michaels surprised her by bowing deeply.

"Wondrous," he murmured, then glanced around the space. He saw Isla and the two men and rushed toward them. After patting her down as though not sure she was real, he turned back to smile at the tall creature.

"Traitor," Hendra murmured under her breath, and yet the sound echoed around the space.

Michaels shook his head and stepped in closer to Isla. "They are more amazing than I could have imagined."

"Yet they have not shown themselves. They have hidden and plotted their way to getting what they want—the power they seek."

"We already have the power," the creature before her said. "We were willing to share, and yet you do not want it."

Hendra opened her mouth and then closed it.

"For yourself perhaps, but not for the people."

"Everything I do is for the people," she said, her voice turning into a screech that ricocheted off the walls. Michaels winced along with several of the soldiers.

"You tell yourself that," Gray murmured, his voice carrying in the strange space. "And yet we all know it isn't true. You have tried to destroy the Rohendra, and in doing so have damaged the Complex. Urgway is breaking apart."

"I feared it would," Michaels said.

"We could save it," the tall creature before her said. His face was turned towards Isla and Gray, although Hendra couldn't be sure where those eyes were looking.

"Will you?" Isla asked. "Or is it part of the plan?"

"You were our plan," he said, stepping forward, and Isla glanced at him.

As the tall creature strode forward, the general came to stand beside Hendra. "He is one of them?" he whispered.

She nodded once, and a duster was pressed into her hand. She doubted she could hit the creature, despite his size, and given that he was Rohen, he might melt and shift to avoid the blast. She glanced at the weapon, noted the settings and thanked her father for insisting on some self-defense training when she was younger. The general was old, and Calder was far away.

Isla was the threat here—she was the reason Hendra had been dragged out. She was the one who had created the rifts with her wife and Calder. She had a way of leading others away from the cause.

Hendra had fired before she'd thought about it. The creature turned slowly, raising a hand, and Calder swung between her and Isla. And then he was gone. Dust settled slowly to the floor, and Isla's horrified face was all she could see.

"He was as we hoped he would be," the creature hummed as Isla dropped to the floor. Gray bent over her, and the general sighed beside her.

Isla stared at the woman standing slack-jawed across the room. She had, in an instant, destroyed the man she had claimed to care for. Isla wasn't as sure what she'd thought about Calder. He had become something else in the past few days—something between the Kalli she had wanted him to be and the man he had been after changing his face to Calder. Now he was gone. She tried to contain the sob, but it built in her chest. Gray pressed his face to hers. It wasn't only her loss, although he had lost his friend many years before.

The Reader before her lowered his hand, and the weapon Hendra turned to study disappeared. She studied her empty hands, her mouth moving as she looked to the general for answers.

"You could have done that before he died," she stammered.

"You could have chosen not to shoot," the Reader said, his voice deep. Isla felt a comfort in it, despite her growing uncertainty. Were they in this to save the people of the Complex as well as the Complex itself, or would the Rohen allow them to destroy each other and claim what was left?

As she looked into his eyes, he crouched down over her. "We need you," he whispered.

"Could you have saved him?" she asked, sniffing in the threatening tears.

He smiled as he ran his old fingers over her cheek. "We need you," he repeated.

She leaned back into Gray, and they stood slowly together. "What happens next?" she asked.

"We await the queen."

"I thought I was already here," Hendra said, her voice carrying across the room although there was something missing, a strength she'd had before perhaps. Isla wondered if she was missing Calder already, or at least regretting her choices.

The Reader smiled, and it made Isla shiver. What might they do to Hendra? They still had their queen to protect, but would they be willing to let Hendra live that long?

"Urgway," Isla said softly, and he turned his attention back to her. "Where are the people?"

He bowed his head to her but didn't answer. Again, she wondered if they might do what was best for them and allow the people of the Complex to die. There were other species out there as well.

"The dust has been destroyed," he said, cocking his head to the side.

Isla nodded. Then he raised a hand and pointed out towards space. They had found a way to destroy the remaining asteroids, then. The Complex was safe from whatever it had been.

"It is time to return," he said.

"To where?" she asked, wondering what was left.

"Where you are needed. To read the words," he murmured, and Gray disappeared in a heartbeat. Isla felt the instant loss of him. "To learn," he said with a smile, raising a hand to Michaels, and he too disappeared. "To do the bidding of the Hendra," he said, his face serious, and the soldiers disappeared. The general stepped in close to the Hendra. "She has her place, and you must protect it." The Hendra looked around at the empty space as the general followed his troops.

Isla worried at where she might be sent. She didn't really have a place outside of helping the Rohen. "There is always a place for you, child." He rested his hand on her shoulder, and she felt the responsibility weigh heavily in that hold. He smiled kindly. "You are more than we could ever need." But when he lifted his hand, she was still in the room.

The Hendra stood alone on the other side, watching them. She had stepped back, but there was nowhere for her to go. Isla couldn't guess at what her place would be in the Complex going forward.

The gentle blue glow of the trees lit up the world around her. If felt like home, although she knew she was far from the forests of Rennet. She stepped towards the closest tree, running her fingers lightly over the texture of the bark.

Why here, she wasn't sure. The place where her nightmares had started, when she had learned of the nature of the world. Although she had always known. Her family, the master, her childhood and the Elite had all been different steps to this one path. She hadn't been making any choices.

She had never escaped what it was she'd been meant to do. Only she had no idea what that was—other than save the Complex. Her laughter echoed around the trees. She had struggled to even save herself, and how many times had she thought she had lost Gray?

The tears that followed were a surprise. There was no way she was walking away this time. She longed for Gray's steadying hold and warm smile. She had only known him a short time, and yet he had quickly grown to be so much.

He would have a different path now. The skills he had with the Rohendra language, the wonder of the words he read coming to life...

"Why here?" Her voice was quiet, and yet it seemed to echo louder than her laughter had.

"This is the centre," a deep voice hummed through her, although it didn't echo from the walls.

"The centre of what?"

"Everything."

Isla looked around then, wishing again that Gray were here to make the trees glow brighter. How it hadn't been destroyed, she wasn't sure, but then they had a way of protecting and hiding themselves. She wondered how had she feared the Hendra could have been any risk at all.

"Her lack of trust would have destroyed us."

"Where is she now?" Isla whispered, wondering what that meant for the Complex going forward.

"The council will guide until our queen is ready."

Isla looked around the space then, searching for what she knew was already gone. A Reader appeared before her, his head bowed and covered by the dark cloth of his cloak. With his arms held close to his chest, he reached forward, bowed low and stepped to the side. Behind him, Hendra rested against a tree—her hand across her belly, her face panicked and her hair dishevelled.

"They will not believe the child hers."

"Those who know the truth will ensure she is what she was meant to be. You have seen it."

Isla nodded, remembering Gray's words and the image of the woman she knew appearing so clearly in the classroom—and then again before the Hendra herself. The woman who, instead of fearing what was to come, saw the image as a sign that she had won.

"She won't accept you," Isla said, looking at the woman who appeared so much older than Isla thought she was. "She won't accept what the Rohendra is."

"She doesn't need to. It is no longer her place."

"What will happen to the child?" Isla asked, unsure why she worried so much. She wasn't going to see the child grow. She wasn't going to be a part of what was to come. Her part was done. She shook her head slowly. "The minister will know what to do."

"He always does," the Reader responded quietly, and Isla felt the assurance that the man would look out for the child, as he did all the gifted.

And yet they were so far away. Three planets stretched between them and a whole lot of space. Isla flinched as cool, smooth, metallic fingers brushed over her face, and she realised she had shed more tears.

"It is not weakness to feel," the Reader whispered, the words washing over her like a warm embrace. She wanted to step into his arms.

"I am sorry to say goodbye," she said.

"We all have purpose," he said. "Yours is just beginning."

"Beginning?" she asked. "I thought my task was done."

"It will never be complete. It is for you to work to ensure the Complex is safe. Your task is to ensure the queen is as she should be. That she understands the connections of the Rohendra Complex."

"She is already Rohendra," Isla said, looking across at the tired woman still unmoving by the tree. "I don't understand."

"You will."

Epilogue

G ray was reading in the study when a strange feeling covered his skin, as though the world had ended and started all in the same instance. He closed the book he was reading and looked at the old man bent over the desk. The candle flickered a gentle orange light across the page he scrawled on, but Gray doubted that he could see any better than if he were writing in the dark. He had never taken the time to really understand the minister's gift. Did he willingly write what came to mind, or was it what Gray had done with his reading initially? He'd just read the words, watching the detail unfold before him, and then the understanding had come.

He closed the book and wandered through the quiet house out into the dark forest that surrounded them.

"It is time," a voice vibrated through him, and he didn't need to ask for what.

He bowed his head and waited.

Isla sat among the children, the large cats prowling the perimeter of the valley as the master whispered stories of the forest and the people. Isla usually felt the loss of those gone as he spoke, but tonight she felt a calm, as though this was where she was meant to be as she waited for what came next. She missed Gray, but she understood he had his own work to do.

The forest seemed to fall silent around them, the night noises that filtered down to them stopped. The cats held their breath, and the children looked to the master.

The silver body of the Rohen reflected the firelight, and Isla climbed slowly to her feet. She was nervous after so long. As the silver form moved towards her, she realised it held something in its arms and someone else followed—a man.

As the Rohen approached, the sounds of the world returned, and with them the sense of the hum of the universe. Had the Rohen been hiding all this time, waiting for the Hendra to leave? Or die—whichever came first.

"Mother," the Rohen whispered, the sound filling her very being. She held out her arms to accept what they offered, and a perfect child was placed in her arms.

"Hendra," she whispered.

"You will know how to raise her," the Rohen returned.

"Why did you not give her to Alice?" Isla asked, her arms closing around the child in fear they would take her away again, and yet Alice was the carer, Alice was the one she should be with.

"Alice has her place, and you have yours, Mother. This is who you are and how you will ensure the safety of the Complex."

The Rohen bowed. As it stepped back, Gray smiled at her and wrapped his arms around them both before helping to lower her back down to the ground. The children crowded in, and the master pulled himself closer.

Isla held the baby securely but gently in her arms. She was so tiny, so precious. Isla wondered if life was going to be as difficult for this child as she feared. Bright blue eyes twinkled at her. Flashes of silver tinged the edges, and Isla knew this child had an advantage. She was Rohendra.

Gray reached in and took the child from her arms without asking, but she didn't stop him. As much as she wanted to watch over the child, she knew he felt the same. He studied her face and traced a finger over her cheek.

"Khalia," he purred, and her eyes shone bright.

"I thought she was only Hendra."

"Not this Hendra, she is known by two names. It means everlasting, and it is what she is."

Acknowledgements

The team at Deranged Doctor Designs (DDD) for absolutely brilliant cover design work and all the marketing extras. Thank you for your support and clear emails around what was needed from me to make the magic happen.

Allison E Wright for wonderful editing work to make my sentences smoother and my intentions clearer.

Special thanks to Yasmin, for taking the time to read my draft and providing ideas to make the story stronger. The support of the Tasmanian Indie Author community and my writerly friends for listening and assisting with all things writing, particularly Danielle, Tara, Nicole, Phyl and Matt.

My parents, Francine and Ken Smith. Amazing, supportive people who I don't thank often enough. Thanks for keeping me grounded and being the best grandparents ever.

As always, Temwa for being my biggest supporter.

About the Author

Georgina Makalani survives life as a servant of the public by hiding in her office at lunch time with dragons, witches, a laptop and a little bit of magic.

For more about Georgina and her books visit her website: www.theflowofink.com